THE BOSTON
BREAKOUT

ROY MacGREGOR

Tundra Books

Text copyright © 2014 by Roy MacGregor

Published in Canada by Tundra Books, a division of Random House of Canada Limited,
One Toronto Street, Suite 300, Toronto, Ontario M5C 2V6

Published in the United States by Tundra Books of Northern New York,
P.O. Box 1030, Plattsburgh, New York 12901

Library of Congress Control Number: 2013953675

Library and Archives Canada Cataloguing in Publication

MacGregor, Roy, 1948-, author
        The Boston breakout / by Roy MacGregor.

(Screech Owls)
Issued in print and electronic formats.
ISBN 978-1-77049-421-3 (pbk.).–ISBN 978-1-77049-426-8 (epub)

        I. Title. II. Series.

PS8575.G84B67 2014   jC813'.54   C2013-906915-1
                                               C2013-906916-X

Designed by Jennifer Lum

www.tundrabooks.com

Printed and bound in the United States of America

1 2 3 4 5 6   19 18 17 16 15 14

This book provided by:

SIGURD F. OLSON
NATURE WRITING AWARD
SIGURD OLSON ENVIRONMENTAL INSTITUTE
Northland College
Ashland, Wisconsin

For Hawkley Robert Roy Dzilums,
who will one day choose his own
team to cheer on . . .

1

Yo! Mom!

Wish you were here (actually, I don't – having way too much fun!). This is a postcard (Coach's idea, not mine). The picture on the front is a statue of Ben Franklin. It's outside the school he quit when he was 10 years old! Soon as I get home, Mom, you and me are going down to Tamarack Public School and I'm handing in my resignation. I'm done with school. *And I mean it! Will explain when I return.*

Your loving son and the Screech Owls' all-time greatest defenseman,

Nish

Wayne Nishikawa licked the stamp and slapped it on the postcard. He stopped to read it to Travis just seconds before he dropped the card into the U.S. Mail box in the hotel lobby. Travis had no time to prevent it from happening. And he couldn't reach down into the box and pull the postcard back – that would be mail theft, a major crime in the United States of America. Travis Lindsay, captain of the Screech Owls peewee hockey team from the little Canadian town of Tamarack, was nothing if not honest.

Travis let his sometimes-best-friend-sometimes-worst-enemy have it. "You idiot!" he yelled at Nish. "You're just going to upset your poor mother. Besides, you can't quit school just like that!"

"Why not? Ben Franklin did. He didn't need

school. I don't need school. Guys like us are too smart for school. School is for dummies."

"Dummies like me, you mean?"

"You said it, not me."

There were tournaments where all you could remember was the hockey. And there were tournaments where the hockey took a backseat. This trip to Boston, Travis had decided, would be one where the hockey played a secondary role.

First, it was summertime. The coach of the Screech Owls, Muck Munro, hated summer hockey. He had long forbidden the Owls to play in any of the weekend tournaments held during July and August. Summer, Muck argued, was for building up your passion for hockey, and you did that by doing something else completely. He wanted the Owls to play other games – lacrosse, for example, or baseball – and to do other things, like swim and camp and take canoe trips. He said this would make them all the more keen for hockey when it started up again in the fall. Travis was pretty sure Muck was right. Besides, Travis loved lacrosse almost as much as hockey and was glad for a summer switch in sports.

So, heading off to a hockey tournament in July was very unusual for the Screech Owls.

Travis knew why they were going. It was because of Muck himself. Not because of Muck's great love of hockey, but because of his passion for history. The coach was always reading history books on their trips. He talked about history when-ever he thought they should know more about a place than just where the dressing rooms were. He'd taken them to the Alamo in Texas, to the field outside Pittsburgh where United Airlines Flight 93 had gone down during the terrorist attacks of 9/11, to the ice surface in Lake Placid where "The Miracle on Ice" had taken place years before any of the Owls had even been born. Muck liked hockey trips to have a point beyond plain hockey.

When the invitation arrived for the Owls to

come to the Paul Revere Peewee Invitational Hockey Tournament, Muck put it to a vote among the Owls' parents and it was unanimous that the team would go. School might be out, but Muck said they'd treat it like a school field trip as much as a hockey tournament. Boston, after all, was where the American Revolution was launched, where Ben Franklin was born, where Paul Revere set out on his horse to warn his countrymen that "The British are coming! The British are coming!"

And Boston was beautiful, a city of world-famous universities, sculls rowing on the Charles River, the Boston Common park, the world-famous New England Aquarium – not to mention the city where the greatest hockey defenseman in history had played – Bobby Orr: number 4.

"I wear number 44," Nish told his teammates, "so I must be ten times as good."

Larry Ulmar, whom everyone called Data, sighed. "That would be *eleven* times as good, Einstein."

Nish snapped back, "Ten, eleven – what's the difference?"

"The difference," said Sarah Cuthbertson, the team's star center, "is that he is Bobby Orr and you are Wayne Nishikawa. That's roughly the difference between night and day."

Nish shot Sarah a raspberry – his usual response to being one-upped.

The trip had come together easily. The kids were all off school. Those involved with lacrosse, baseball, football, swimming lessons or camp were all given permission to miss the week. Only a few of the parents would be coming along, but they were traveling on their own. For the Owls themselves, Mr. Dillinger, the team's beloved manager, had the old team bus – a secondhand school bus – up and running as good as ever.

With Mr. D at the wheel and Muck lost in a huge book about the Boston Tea Party, the Owls had come over the Thousand Islands Bridge near Kingston on a gorgeous bright morning and headed across Upstate New York. They took the ferry across Lake Champlain, Nish screaming all the way that the tiny waves were making him seasick. Over and over, he yelled, "I'M GONNA HURL!"

Across Vermont, down through New Hampshire, and on into Massachusetts the old bus rumbled. They stopped for pee breaks and for one Stupid Stop, which meant Mr. D handed out small American bills to the players, with instructions to "Buy something completely silly and totally useless." Nish used his money to buy a little plastic disc launcher and spent the rest of the trip annoying everyone on the bus by shooting tiny flying saucers at them while they were sleeping.

They checked into their hotel – the Marriott Long Wharf, right next to the New England Aquarium – and Muck and Mr. D gave them a half hour to "freshen up" before meeting down in the lobby for something "very special."

Nish's idea of freshening up differed from that of Travis and their two roommates: Lars Johanssen, the little Swedish-born defenseman, and Wilson Kelly, also a defenseman. Wilson had been born in Regina, Saskatchewan, but maintained he would one day play hockey in the Olympics for Team Jamaica, if Jamaica ever got a hockey team, because both his parents had come from there. Wilson and

Lars carefully emptied out their suitcases, just as Travis had done, and began dividing up the drawers in the dresser so they wouldn't be getting things like socks and underwear mixed up. They were almost done when Nish walked into the room, zipped open his suitcase, turned it upside down so the contents landed on the floor, then tossed the empty case in a corner. He plopped down on a bed, reached for the remote, and immediately began surfing channels in the hope that Muck and Mr. D hadn't asked the front desk to block the adult movie channel. Muck and Mr. D had, however; they knew Nish too well.

A half hour later, all the Owls – Travis, Nish, Lars, Wilson, Data, Sarah, Dmitri Yakushev, Samantha Bennett, Simon Milliken, Derek Dillinger, Jeremy Weathers, Jenny Staples, Jesse Highboy, Andy Higgins, Gordie Griffith, and Fahd Noorizadeh – gathered in the lobby of the hotel. Muck and Mr. D were waiting for them with an announcement.

"We're going to walk the Freedom Trail," Muck said.

"Can't we drive it?" Nish whined.

Muck ignored the comment and continued. "You're going to see where the United States was born. Mr. D here has arranged for a guide, and we're all going to spend the afternoon seeing some of the most historical sites in Boston. So let's head out. It's a long walk on a hot day."

"Don't they have a video version?" Nish asked.

Muck said nothing. He didn't need to. His stare froze Nish on the spot.

2

The tour guide was wonderful. Dressed in period costume – blue waistcoat, wide-brimmed hat, long stockings, leather shoes with gleaming French buckles, a powder bag slung over his right shoulder – he was full of fascinating tales. They set out across the gorgeous green Boston Common toward the Massachusetts State House. All along the walk, he told them how this was where the colonists in America first rose up against British rule and British taxes and where American independence was born.

He took them to the Granary Burying Ground nearby and showed them the graves of Paul Revere, Samuel Adams ("I thought he was a beer," Nish hissed behind Travis's ear), and John Hancock, whose flowery signature was on the Declaration of Independence.

Travis blushed to recall his own efforts to create a fancy signature. At the back of the little scrapbook he kept for newspaper stories about the Owls that he clipped from the *Tamarack Weekly* he had reserved several pages for practicing autographs. He must have tried forty or fifty different styles before he settled on one that included a long loop in the *Y*, the last letter of his name, and tucked inside the loop was a carefully drawn *7* – his number, and the number once worn by his father's distant cousin, "Terrible" Ted Lindsay, when Ted Lindsay was a star with Gordie Howe and the Detroit Red Wings.

The Owls took pictures of the various graves and monuments. Wilson asked Travis to take a photo of him standing beside a tiny little gravestone off to the side of the huge monument to John Hancock. The simple marker said "Frank – Servant to John Hancock." The guide had explained that Frank was a slave who was owned by the Hancock family. Frank was so beloved by the Hancocks that they got special permission to bury him here, beside his master, rather than in the burial ground designated for slaves.

"They didn't even give him a last name," said Wilson, his eyes tearing up for someone he'd never known. "Just *Frank*. Like he was the family dog or something."

Travis said nothing. He took the photo for Wilson and handed the camera back. What could he say? The world was sometimes such a mystifying place.

The group moved down a side street to Boston Latin School, which the guide said was "the first public school in the United States. It dates from 1635. It was a school nearly four hundred years ago – and it remains a school today."

The guide named a long list of people who had gone to the school, most of them unfamiliar to Travis. Presidents of Harvard University had gone here. Several state governors had gone to school here. And Ben Franklin had once been a student here.

"Benjamin Franklin," the guide said, "may have been the smartest American ever. He was a great writer and a newspaper editor and publisher. He was an accomplished musician. He signed the Declaration of Independence. He served as United States ambassador to France. He was a chess master and spoke fluent French and Italian as well as English. He studied electricity. He invented the lightning rod and bifocal glasses. He was an absolute genius, no doubt, but there is something even more unusual about Ben Franklin. It has to do with his statue standing here at this very school. Can anyone tell me what it is?"

The Owls mumbled among themselves and guessed. Fahd thought Franklin had "invented" electricity and several of the players agreed, but the guide said no, he didn't invent electricity, but it was true that Ben Franklin flew a kite in a lightning storm to study the behavior of electricity. Sam thought maybe he had invented the camera, but the guide shook his head and smiled.

"No," he said. "It's got something to do with this school."

Muck could hold his answer in no longer. "He dropped out."

The guide raised an eyebrow in appreciation. "You knew!" he said to Muck, who appeared to blush. "You're right!

"Benjamin Franklin, the smartest man in America, despised school," the guide said to the delighted Owls. "His family was poor. His father was a candle-maker."

"What did his mother do?" Sarah asked.

The guide laughed. "She *survived*. Mrs. Franklin had seventeen children. Little Ben was her fifteenth. But the family recognized that he was brilliant beyond his years, and somehow they got the money together to enroll him here. It was then called the South Grammar School. But he hated it."

"How old was he when he quit?" Fahd asked.

"Ten," the guide said. "When he was ten years

old, he dropped out and never again attended a single day of school."

"I'm twelve," Nish said. "That means I've already wasted two years of my life."

The guide laughed and moved on. Nearby was a life-size statue of a donkey, symbol of the Democratic Party.

Nish climbed onto its back and asked Fahd to take his picture.

"Perfect," Sam pronounced. "A total ass sitting on an ass."

But the idea had lodged in Nish's brain. They spent the rest of the afternoon visiting the various sites along the Freedom Trail: Faneuil Hall, Paul Revere's house, the Bunker Hill monument, and, all the way out along the harbor, the USS *Constitution*, the famous three-masted warship that had won so many battles during the War of 1812.

The Owls had never seen Muck so happy. After the tour, their coach took them to a nearby souvenir store and told them all to pick out postcards and he would pay for them.

The Owls all thought the cards were just for themselves, small souvenirs of the afternoon, but Muck had other ideas.

"We're going back to the hotel, and you are all going to send your card home with a message for the parents who couldn't come on the trip. I want them to know you're not just wasting your time and their money while you're here in Boston. We want them to know you might be learning something as well."

Some of the Owls groaned. They didn't want to write postcards. They wanted to try the hotel pool.

"No one sends postcards," Nish said. "Why can't we just text them to let them know we're okay?"

Muck sent a withering stare at the mouthy defenseman.

An hour later, Nish had his postcard written, addressed, and stamped. And before Travis could stop it, the message was in the mail and on its way to poor, suffering Mrs. Nishikawa, who was about to find out that her only son had decided to quit school.

3

The Owls' first game was scheduled for the Boston Bruins' practice arena in nearby Wilmington. Mr. D pulled up the old team bus outside the suburban rink. The bus burped and backfired in a cloud of black exhaust as the engine died. Mr. D grasped his nose and made a face as if the old bus had just passed wind.

Travis caught his own reflection in the side mirror that the driver used for backing up. His first thought was that he had never seen himself reflected there before. Could he be getting taller? *Finally?*

Travis's mother had told him he worried unnecessarily about his size. "Lindsay men are late bloomers," she said. "You'll grow taller than your father, just you wait and see."

Travis hoped so. His father was tall, taller than most of the other fathers of his teammates, but why did he have to "wait and see"? Why couldn't he grow now, so he could stop worrying about it?

He could see he was changing. His face was a little longer. His hair was close-cut now, and thanks to the summer sun it was more blond than it was in hockey season. Travis looked around at his teammates to see if they, too, were changing. Sarah's hair was like gold. It even seemed to sparkle. Travis couldn't tell if she looked different. Sam's hair was as red as ever. Jesse Highboy was maybe broader at the shoulders. Little Simon Milliken was finally catching up to the rest. Only Nish seemed not to have changed one bit: still wider than any of the others, still slopping stuff into his hair so he could style it high like his idol, Elvis Presley. Still with a face that couldn't hide an emotion even if you pulled a brown paper bag over it. That face – beet red during games, redder yet when embarrassed, twisting and churning with whatever mad plan or crazy thought was passing through it – was pure Nish. His signature. No flowery loop or number 44 required.

The Owls were thrilled to think that the Boston Bruins, Stanley Cup champions, had sat in the very stalls they would be sitting in. They would be skating on the same ice as Bruins captain Zdeno Chara, hockey's tallest player at six foot nine. And if they went all the way to the final of the Paul Revere tournament, they would play for the championship in the Boston TD Garden itself, the rink where all the great stars of the NHL – Sidney Crosby, Steven Stamkos, Taylor Hall, Alexander Ovechkin, and dozens of others – had played. It was not the old Boston Garden, where Bobby Orr had practically reinvented the way defense was played in hockey, but it was close. It was a true NHL hockey rink, and that was what mattered most.

There had been no time for practice sessions. The tournament was beginning immediately so that all games could be fitted in before the championship round on the weekend. First up against the Screech Owls would be the Chicago Young Blackhawks, one of the top peewee teams in the country.

The Owls and the Young Blackhawks had met before, at the Big Apple tournament in New York City. Travis remembered that they had been a tough team to play, smart and quick and well-coached. The Owls had only got past them thanks to a brilliant play by Nish at the blue line. Nish had twisted and danced his way in with the puck and then dished off at the last moment to Travis, who scored the winner in a close 3–2 game.

Travis also remembered the championship game in that tournament. Again, it was the Nish show. The Owls had come back all the way to even the score against the State Selects, and Nish had then settled the game, scoring a truly ridiculous goal by sticking his stick between his legs and roofing the puck. Nish had seen an old YouTube clip of

Mario Lemieux doing this for the Pittsburgh Penguins and vowed he'd do the same. Muck was not amused – the Owls' coach hated "showboaters" – but the team had been delighted. They'd won the championship.

Travis dressed slowly. After several weeks away from the ice, he wanted to savor his return. He put his gear on precisely as always, first right side then left – shin pads, socks, shoulder pads, elbow pads, skates – then kissed the inside of his jersey as the Screech Owls crest and the letter *C* on the outside slipped over his head and shoulders. He placed the helmet over his head, snapped the face shield in place, tucked on his gloves, grabbed his stick – and was set.

So, too, were the other Owls. Sarah was concentrating so fiercely on her hands it seemed she might burn them with X-ray vision. And Nish was doubled over, his head between his padded knees as he stared hard, hard, hard at the floor. Each Screech Owl had his or her own special ritual. Each respected the others' little quirks, even if, as in the case of Nish, it was hard to keep a straight face when watching them get ready to play.

The ice felt slightly alien. There was no way, Travis knew, that he would feel as comfortable as he did mid-season, when it seemed his feet and skates had melded together as a natural part of his body. He never thought about skating then. Now he had to concentrate on his stride. He could feel unfamiliar muscles – "hockey muscles," Muck called them – straining into action. It was almost as if he'd rusted up while being off the ice.

The Young Blackhawks had clearly been playing summer hockey. The Owls sensed it immediately in the warm-up. They seemed to be in a higher gear and brimming with confidence.

"I'd love to wipe the smiles off those smug faces," Nish hissed as he and Travis moved in on Jenny Staples to tap her pads and goalposts. It was a pregame ritual that Jenny insisted be followed exactly the same each time: Nish tapped one pad, Travis the other; Nish bumped one post with his fist, Travis the other.

Hockey rituals fascinated Travis. He'd once read a book called *A Loonie for Luck* about the Canadian gold-medal victory at the Salt Lake City Olympics. The book told the story about a "lucky loonie," a one-dollar coin that Canadian ice-maker Trent Evans secretly buried at center ice to inspire the men's and women's hockey teams on their way to the gold, but it also included other stories of weird hockey superstitions.

When Gretzky played, he used to put baby powder between his stick blade and tape to "soften" his passes. Hall of Famer Phil Esposito wouldn't stay in any hotel room that had the number 13 in it, and he kept so many rabbits' feet and lucky charms hanging in his stall he could barely find his equipment. Bobby Orr never wore socks in his skates. But Travis's all-time favorite concerned a player named Bruce Gardiner who had fallen into a terrible scoring slump while with the Ottawa Senators. Gardiner became so frustrated with his lack of goals that once, between periods, he took his stick into the washroom, placed the blade of his stick into the toilet bowl – and flushed. He immediately went out and scored. Soon all of the Senators were "flushing" their sticks before games.

Travis had his own little tics. He had to kiss the inside of his jersey. He had to hit the crossbar with a warm-up shot. Jenny had to have her shin pads and posts tapped. Nish had to put his head between his knees. Sarah and Sam had a secret message they exchanged just before heading onto the ice. They refused to let anyone else know what it was for fear it would "break the spell." Travis suspected that even Muck was superstitious. The Screech Owls' coach insisted on wearing his scruffy old hockey jacket behind the bench when virtually every other peewee coach wore a jacket and tie as if they were in the NHL.

So when Travis missed the crossbar in the warm-up, he hoped it didn't mean anything.

It turned out it did. Nish had wanted to "wipe the smiles" off the faces of the Young Blackhawks, but quite the opposite happened. By game's end, the team in Blackhawks red and black was whooping and hollering and openly laughing. They had out-skated, outplayed, outhustled, and outscored the Screech Owls 9–2.

Travis could not recall the Owls ever getting such a severe whipping. They had lost many games, but usually it was close. This was a rout – a "spank-ing," as they said in hockey.

It had gone wrong from the beginning. Sarah lost the opening face-off – unusual in itself, as she prided herself on gaining that very first puck of the game – and Dmitri, racing in alone after Sarah retrieved the puck and sent a long pass up the right wing to set him free, missed on his familiar fore-hand fake to be followed by a backhand to the roof. The puck didn't even tick off a post or the crossbar before it pinged into the glass behind the Young Blackhawks' net.

Fahd scored in the first period on a shot that he'd intended as a pass to Andy Higgins but instead deflected off a defenseman's skate and into the far side of the net. And Sam scored on a shot from the point that bounced once before reaching the goalie and took a weird turn to the right as the goaltender positioned himself to handle the bounce.

Two goals from the defense; none from the forwards. The Owls' top line of Travis, Sarah, and Dmitri could not recall a time when they'd been shut down so completely. None of them could perform against their opponents' heavy checking. They barely managed to get the puck into the Blackhawks' end.

The most spectacular Owls play of the game had been pure disaster. Nish took the puck behind his own net, banked a pass to himself off the back boards as a checker flew past him, then broke out hard up the right side. At the blue line, he fed a pass across to Travis, who used the give-and-go to get the puck right back to Nish as the big Owls' defenseman blew past center ice.

Nish perfectly split the Young Blackhawks' defense as he came in, leaping high at one point to clear their sticks as both defenders fell.

He was in alone. Which was when he tried his "showboat" play of putting his stick through his own legs for the spectacular Mario Lemieux shot.

Only it didn't work. Nish ended up tripping himself and crashed to the ice. He slammed into the backboards, where he lay moaning while the puck trickled harmlessly off into the other corner.

The referee blew the play down, thinking Nish might be badly hurt.

"Give him a penalty for tripping himself!" one of the Young Blackhawks shouted from the opposition bench.

Travis could hear the other team howling with laughter. His face burned with more than the exertion of playing.

Now he, too, wanted to "wipe the smiles" off those smug laughing faces.

Muck took it philosophically. The Owls all knew their coach would be furious at the Young Blackhawks' coaching staff for allowing their team to run up the score – in Muck's opinion, one of the greatest sins in hockey – but he wasn't saying anything to them about that. If he had something to say, he would say it privately to the Young Blackhawks' head coach.

"You can't win or lose a tournament in the first game," Muck told his exhausted team in the dressing room. "It's over and done with. Forgotten. They have their hockey muscles from playing all summer. You don't. It's as simple as that."

Muck said no more. He stepped outside the dressing room and closed the door, leaving his team with their own thoughts.

And what thoughts they were. As captain, Travis felt he had failed his entire team. As the team's top playmaker, Sarah felt she had failed her linemates. As the team's greatest player and future Hall of Famer (his opinion, not necessarily shared by his teammates), Nish felt he had made a perfect ass of himself when he could have put the Owls back in the game.

Mr. D quietly went about packing up his skate-sharpening equipment, tape bag, toolbox, and first-aid kit. He whistled softly to himself, his thick mustache moving to its own rhythm as his lips worked through an old rock 'n' roll song.

The Owls packed their bags and set out their sweaty underwear for washing back at the hotel.

Still no one said anything. What was there to say?

It was Mr. D who finally spoke. With a single sentence, he changed both the subject and the mood.

"Second thing in the morning," Mr. D said, his mustache curling into a wide smile, "we're all going to the New England Aquarium."

"What do we do first thing in the morning?" Fahd asked.

Mr. D kicked at the pile of laundry, making a face at it.

"We wash Nishikawa's underwear," he said, turning to Nish with a sly grin.

"Bad enough you stunk out there. You don't need to stink up the place in here as well."

4

The Screech Owls had never seen anything quite like the New England Aquarium. It was a short walk from their hotel along a small park and then a wide boardwalk that wrapped around the huge gray aquarium building. The aquarium looked like an airplane hangar and an art gallery at the same time, a massive building, without windows for the most part, but with a spectacular glass entrance with a sweeping glass-and-steel roof over the front. On the other side of the walkway, the water of Boston Harbor sparkled in the morning sun.

Nish had other plans. He told Muck and Mr. D he wanted to go out to Boston College, where football quarterback Doug Flutie – who later became a star in the Canadian Football League – had made his famous Hail Mary pass to win a game over Miami in the final seconds, throwing the ball so high and far that only blind luck had made it land in the hands of a Boston College player. Nish wanted to head for Fenway Park, where baseball's Red Sox were having a home stand against the Toronto Blue Jays. He wanted to detour by the Ben Franklin statue to pay his respects and thank the Founding Father for inspiring him to quit school. He wanted to board one of the many Super Duck tours – weird-looking yellow buses that took tourists along the streets and then drove right into the harbor and kept on going. He wanted to do everything, it seemed, except actually *learn* something.

"This will be educational," Travis had argued. He also thought, though he didn't say it, that it would bring the Owls back to their old, positive selves. They were still crushed by the result of their opening game.

Nish quickly dismissed him. "I'm done with education. You saw the postcard. I've got more education than Ben Franklin – so what can school do for me?"

"You're impossible," Sarah pitched in.

"I'm a genius," Nish shot back. "I don't need no more school."

"You don't need *any* more school," Sam corrected.

"That's right," Nish said, grinning proudly. "Glad you agree."

Before they reached the aquarium, Mr. D, who was leading the adventure, gathered the Owls together in the small park. He had to wait a while for Nish, who had dragged his feet the whole way. The boardwalk was swarming with tourists, and there were long lineups for tickets into the aquarium.

An area on the side of the aquarium closest to the harbor had been cordoned off with yellow

DO NOT CROSS tape and metal barricades. Behind the tape, scaffolding had been erected, and several construction workers were moving about. It appeared they were punching through the wall to make a new entrance or delivery area for the huge building.

The construction work sort of ruined the opportunity for a good photograph of the aquarium, but Travis took one anyway. His grandparents, who had all sorts of books at their cottage on fish and water life, would want to see everything when he got back to Tamarack.

Beyond the construction area, along a narrow strip between the building and the water, a large group of adults had gathered. Some held signs that they kept down at their feet. They seemed to be listening intently to someone, a person dressed in what appeared to be a penguin costume. Once in a while, Travis thought he could hear the speaker shouting. It was a woman's voice, but Travis was unable to make out what she was saying over the sound of traffic in the street just behind.

Something about the group suggested they weren't there to see the exhibits. But Travis had no time to find out what their purpose was. The Owls were ready to head into the aquarium.

"We've already got tickets," Mr. D announced, beginning to hand them into the reaching hands of the various Owls. "We are to meet our guide at the harbor seal exhibit at the front of the building."

The harbor seals were the first thing visitors encountered at the aquarium. They were both outside and inside, with their own pool, and the Owls were being granted access to the inside of their display area.

The Owls' guide, Jocelyn, told them all about the playful creatures as the seals seemed to dance underwater to entertain the visitors, blowing bubbles and waving at the little children pressing their faces to the glass.

Jocelyn introduced the Owls to Chacoda, a seal that she claimed could "talk." Chacoda said something that sounded very much like "How are you?" when Jocelyn made a great show of introducing him to Simon Milliken, who seemed uneasy at being singled out for special attention.

Chacoda, the guide explained, was the grandson

of Hoover, the most famous harbor seal of all time. Hoover had come to the aquarium at the age of four months, having been rescued as a baby and kept by a family in their bathtub.

"He could say his own name," said Jocelyn. "And he knew all sorts of phrases, like 'Get outta here!' and 'How are ya?' And he said it with a Maine accent, just like the family that rescued him!"

Hoover had lived to the great old age of twenty-four and for years was studied by scientists, who could never quite figure out how the seal came to sound so much like a human. He had been so famous in Boston that when he died the newspapers ran his obituary, as if Hoover had been a real person. "And to us, here at the New England Aquarium, he was," said Jocelyn.

"*Get outta here!*" hissed Nish.

All the Owls stared daggers at him. Nish blushed and put on his innocent choirboy look, holding out his hands, palms up, as if he couldn't understand why they were glaring at him.

The group went inside, where Jocelyn directed them toward the large penguin exhibit that took up most of the first floor of the building. Travis thought the display looked amazing. There were large swimming areas, where visitors could watch the penguins dive; smaller tidal pools, where the penguins could wade around in the water; and rock structures they could climb upon. Some of the penguins were called rockhoppers, and the Owls delighted in watching them leap about the rocks, the long yellow feathers on their heads flapping as they jumped.

Jocelyn told them that about one hundred penguins lived at the aquarium – from large emperor penguins to little tiny blue ones. She pointed to one group of birds that seemed to be braying like donkeys about something. "Those are African penguins," she said, "also known as jackass penguins because of that sound."

"How nice," Sam whispered loudly in Sarah's direction, "a bird for Nish."

Travis was glad to see his teammates returning to normal – even if it meant taking shots at Nish. It showed they weren't so upset anymore at the terrible beating they had taken from the Chicago Young Blackhawks. Muck had always taught them,

"You *move on* from a loss – you can't go back and play it again." But this had been more than a loss. It was a humiliation, and the Owls weren't used to being humiliated on the ice.

Jocelyn pointed to Sam and asked her to step forward. Sam – a little red-faced, thinking she was about to get into trouble – did as she was asked. But it was not to be told to smarten up and lay off Nish. Sam was to go right down into the penguin exhibit with one of the handlers and experience something very special.

Sam seemed bewildered, but one of the workers who took care of the penguins came up and took her hand and guided her into the exhibit. Tourists all around snapped photographs of the little girl from the hockey team who was getting to join the penguins.

"We have a new baby," the worker told her. He reached down and very carefully pulled a tiny penguin out from behind a rock.

"Can I hold it?" Sam asked.

The handler shook his head. "We want you to take off your shoes. It's shallow here, so your shorts won't get wet. We want you to sit by the penguin a moment and then do nothing but get up and begin walking, very slowly, across this tidal pool to the far side. Okay? And keep changing direction as you go?"

"O-k-kay," Sam stuttered, unsure what was going to happen.

The worker stepped away, and Sam settled down near the baby penguin for a while, then got up and slowly began moving across the shallow pond.

The baby penguin squawked and followed, hurrying to catch up.

The worker and Jocelyn laughed. Every turn that Sam made, the penguin followed. Sam could not get away from the little bird. If Sam stopped, the penguin stopped with her. If she started up, the penguin started up again, too. Sam zigged, the penguin zigged. Sam zagged, the penguin zagged. It was hilarious to watch.

Eventually, the worker went over, scooped up the little bird and placed it back where it had been. He then took Sam's hand and helped her out of the water and back up the rocks to where she could step out of the exhibit again and join her teammates.

"Ladies and gentlemen," the worker said in a rather theatrical manner, "may I present to you Mother Penguin!"

Everyone laughed at Sam's new name.

"What you just saw was a baby penguin *imprinting*," the worker said. "The first creature he sees, he assumes it's his mother, and he'll follow his mother anywhere."

"Where's its real mother?" Fahd asked.

"This egg was incubated," the worker said. "Naturally, it's far better to have the mother and father care for the egg until it hatches, but once in a while an egg is abandoned or, in the wild, an accident happens to one or both parents, leaving the egg to freeze in the cold. So, sometimes, the staff here have to become the orphan's 'mother' for a while.

"We release the orphans into the exhibit and they imprint on the first bird – or, in this case, young lady – they come across."

"So sweet," said Sarah, sighing.

"I love him!" Sam said, looking back at her "baby."

"*I'm gonna hurl*," someone hissed from the back of the gathering.

Travis didn't need to turn to know who it was.

With Jocelyn guiding them, the Owls walked up a wide ramp that circled like a corkscrew around the largest tank any of them had ever seen.

"This tank is over four stories high," Jocelyn told them. "It holds more than two hundred thousand gallons of water. That's nearly one million, seven hundred thousand pounds pressing on the glass, about ten full-size swimming pools' worth of water, so you can just imagine how strong it has to be to withstand that kind of pressure."

Nish, unable to resist, dashed from the group, leaped in the air, and butt-checked the glass as if he'd just scored one of his glory goals. He bounced off the glass like a housefly off a kitchen window. The other Owls laughed at him as he rolled partway down the ramp.

"See what I mean?" Jocelyn told them, laughing herself. "That glass is strong as a wall."

They stopped at various points and watched an

endless parade of sea creatures swim by: large groupers, stingrays, sand sharks, barracuda, moray eels, flashing schools of herring, traveling in perfect formation, and hundreds of exquisitely colored reef fish.

"How many creatures are in there?" Fahd asked.

"About six hundred," Jocelyn answered, "but we're never quite sure. We do a census about once a year – in fact, we're starting it tomorrow – where divers go right into the tank and count them. Usually it's about six hundred, give or take several dozen."

Jocelyn positioned herself so she could see what creatures were coming. "Get ready for a surprise," she announced.

"What?" several of the Owls shouted.

Instantly, it was apparent what was coming – the largest turtle any of them had ever seen drifted by, moving slowly, deliberately, and effortlessly, almost as if it were on a space walk rather than swimming through water.

"What is *that*?" Jesse asked.

"That's Myrtle, queen of the aquarium," Jocelyn laughed. "She's a green sea turtle, and she's been here for more than fifty years. No one knows how old she really is. We weighed her once, though — and she's almost six hundred pounds."

"About Nish's size," Sam whispered to Sarah.

Nish shot them both a raspberry.

"Isn't it dangerous in there?" asked Lars. "You've got eels and sharks and all sorts of things."

Jocelyn smiled. "We send divers into the tank every day," she said. "If you come down to the lower windows, you'll see them playing with the sand sharks right now."

"*Playing?*" Derek said, incredulous.

"Sure," Jocelyn said. She led them down the ramp to where, indeed, two divers inside the tank were playing with a very large sand shark. "They all know each other. The sharks are happy to see the divers, and for a very good reason. Anyone know what that is?"

Jeremy answered. "Food?"

"Right. They carry down some of the food the sharks like best. So the sharks look forward to their visits."

"Aren't they food themselves?" Nish asked.

"Sand sharks are fine," Jocelyn answered. "We

keep the dangerous sea animals in separate areas. Like the poison dart frog and certain jellyfish you wouldn't want to touch. You'll see them in different sections of the aquarium. We even have a special tank where you can pet eels if you like."

"*No way!*" Nish shouted.

"The eels love it," Jocelyn answered. "They like people."

"Not this people, they wouldn't," Nish said.

"Then the eels are just like us," said Sam, giggling.

The guide caught on that Nish was – well – a bit different from his teammates.

"What's your name?" Jocelyn asked.

"Wayne Nishikawa," Nish answered.

"Call him Nish," Sam said. "We all do."

"Okay, Nish," Jocelyn continued. "Would you mind helping me out with our next exhibit?"

"What is it?" Nish asked.

"You'll see."

The guide took the Owls over to a large open tank off to one side of the giant aquarium building. It was filled with what looked at first like floating kites.

"There are sixteen different species of rays and sharks in this tank," Jocelyn said. "And they all like to be petted."

"*Petted?*" several of the Screech Owls asked at once. Surely Jocelyn was pulling their legs. *Petted? Sharks and rays you could *pet*?

"Come over here, Nish," Jocelyn commanded, moving to the side of the tank.

"No way!"

"C'mon," she laughed. "I don't bite."

"But *they* do!"

"No, they won't. Really. Come here."

Nish's face twisted into that tortured tomato that the Owls knew so well. He moved reluctantly to the side of the tank. Jocelyn reached out and took his arm. He snapped his hand fearfully away from her. She reached again, and this time he let her take it.

With Jocelyn guiding his hand, Nish was able to reach into the tank, where, to the Owls' amazement, a number of rays had come over and seemed to be lifting their "wings" in an effort to reach back.

Nish let Jocelyn guide his hand over the wings. "They're smooth!" he said, surprised.

"Now we'll try touching a shark," she said.

"No way! I'd *die* first!"

"Don't be silly, Nish," Jocelyn said, guiding his hand this time toward the flat head of a small shark that had twisted its way through the mass of rays. "This shark is very friendly. It's a kind of hammerhead shark."

Sam and Sarah looked at each other and nodded.

"Maybe Nish should give it a headbutt," Sam said.

5

The light blinded Travis – the noise all but deafened him.

The Screech Owls had just come out of the New England Aquarium into the brilliant sunlight of a July noon hour. The sun stabbing into Travis's eyes caused him to blink until he could regain focus. The noise, however, remained the same: thunder-like and echoing. Made by people shouting angrily.

There was a rally going on. The broad walkway

to the aquarium was filled with two hundred or more protesters holding up placards and shaking them while several television crews filmed.

"*Free the penguins!*" they shouted.

"*Close down the NEA prison!*"

"*Put the scientists on display, not the sharks!*"

"*Drain the tanks!*"

"*Release the penguins!*"

A platform and microphone had been set up to one side. Beside the platform, the woman in the penguin costume was conferring with a couple of other protesters.

"What's this all about?" Sarah asked.

"Animal rights protest, I suppose," said Data. "They think zoos should be shut down and the animals released back to nature. I guess it's the same with aquariums."

Men and women wearing buttons saying "Free the Penguins" were walking about the boardwalk, handing out leaflets. Nish waved them away when two of them approached the Owls, but Sam stepped forward and took one. A woman held out a leaflet in Travis's direction; being too polite to refuse it,

Travis took it, folded it carefully, and stuffed it in his back pocket.

The woman dressed in the penguin suit was now at the microphone. Feedback screeched loudly over the speakers, and a man wearing earphones at a nearby control panel quickly turned some dials. Instantly, the area filled with the booming, echoing voice of the woman in the penguin suit.

"*We are here today in support of those in captivity!*" she shouted. "*We are the voice of the prisoners of the New England Aquarium. We are here to see justice served, to see those who belong to the sea returned to the sea.*"

The woman in the penguin suit went on about the rights of animals to live their lives as nature intended. She spoke about how penguins that were hatched in the aquarium were fooled into believing human beings were their parents. "*How ridiculous is that?*" she shouted. "*How wrong is that?*"

The Owls stood there, watching and listening, Mr. D checking his watch every minute or so. It was fascinating. The Owls had never heard anything like it.

After the penguin woman, a man talked about how chickens were raised in mass poultry farms where their captors cut off their beaks so they couldn't peck each other to death. He talked about how geese were force-fed so that their livers swelled up, and how the bloated livers were used to create a gourmet dish called pâté. Another man talked about how cows and pigs never saw the light of day, never felt sunshine on their bodies or grass under their feet. They were kept in "animal prison cells" where food was pumped in one end and waste material pumped out the other. "Meat factories," he called them.

"Sick," said Fahd.

"What's that got to do with the aquarium?" Sarah asked. "The animals we saw inside were wonderfully well cared for and weren't going to be eaten by anyone – or anything, for that matter."

"Still," added Sam, "it's wrong, no matter how you look at it. What right do we have to decide the fate of others? Just because we're humans doesn't mean we get to do whatever we want to other animals."

"I'd like to *eat* another animal right about now," said Nish. "Maybe some KFC without the beaks!"

Sam turned furiously on Nish, her eyes blazing.

"How would *you* like to be raised in a cage?" she shouted.

"I have been," Nish shot back. "It's called *school* – and I'm about to break free!"

This time it was Sam who blew a raspberry at Nish – but at the same time she was clearly starting to cry.

"Okay, okay, okay," Mr. D said, bringing an end to the exchange between Nish and Sam. "We've got a lunch to make and a game to play."

"What's for lunch?" Nish asked. "I'm in the mood for seafood."

Travis reached out and pinched the inside of Nish's arm. A signal for him to cool it. He was going too far.

But it was too late. Sam was running ahead of the rest of the Owls, and Travis could tell she was truly upset.

6

C lang!

"*Yes!*" Travis shouted to himself, the sound contained inside his face mask. He had just cranked his first shot of the warm-up off the crossbar, the puck sailing high into the wall of glass behind Jeremy Weathers's net.

This one was going to be different.

The Screech Owls were again at the Wilmington arena, this time up against the Pittsburgh River Rats, a team they knew only too well. The two teams had met previously at the Peewee Winter Classic played outdoors at Heinz Field in the River Rats' home city.

It was the big winger on the Pittsburgh side who had drilled Travis headfirst into the boards in Game 1 of that tournament. The hit had given Travis a concussion. Travis didn't like to remember it: the pain of the hit, the unshakable sense of being awake in a dream, the headaches, the way he had to avoid light and sound – but mostly being unable to play until cleared by the doctor. He never wished to go through an experience like that again.

Travis scanned the opposition during their warm-up. He couldn't see the big player who had hurt him. Sarah, it turned out, had been doing the same and also noticed the player's absence.

"Mr. D says that the guy felt so bad about causing the accident, he quit hockey for good," Sarah said, as she and Travis lined up to take practice shots at Jeremy and Jenny.

Travis could only nod. It was too emotional for him to say anything. He hated being the reason someone had given up this wonderful game. The winger hadn't deliberately set out to hurt him.

He changed the topic. "I can skate a lot better today," he told Sarah.

He could see her smile behind her face mask. "Me, too," she said. "Feels good."

The Owls were not the same team that had been thrashed the day before by the Young Blackhawks. They had jump this time, and speed, and their timing was coming back fast. Travis no longer had to think about his skating. He was thinking about where he should be and what he would do when he got there. He was "thinking the game," as Muck always said they needed to, and no longer "thinking the player" – himself.

Lars led the Owls' first rush against the River Rats. He flew out of his own end with the puck dancing on his stick as if it were attached by invisible strings, up to center, where he dished off to Dmitri on his right, who skated over the opposition blue line but left the puck sitting right on the line for Sarah to pick up as she came up behind him with speed.

Sarah threw a pass over to Travis, the puck flying over the reaching sticks of the Rats' defense, to be knocked down by Travis with a quick chop. He kicked the puck ahead to his stick blade, faked a shot at the goaltender, but instead twisted a pass back to Lars, still coming with the rush.

Lars had an empty net to fire at.

1–0, Owls.

The Pittsburgh team wasn't ready to lie down so the Owls could feel better with a comeback win. They were a good team. They had replaced the big winger with a highly skilled little guy who could outrace every Owl but Sarah and Dmitri.

Early in the second period, the little River Rat came down Travis's side and sent himself a perfect pass by bouncing the puck off the boards and picking it up again after he'd raced around Travis.

Travis turned and gave chase, furious at himself for getting caught in such a predictable play, but he stood no chance of catching the little speedster.

Up ahead he saw Nish coming cross-ice fast. Nish didn't have the speed of Dmitri or Sarah, but in times of great need he could move quickly.

Nish left his feet! He wasn't falling – he was *flying*. He hurled himself into the air and seemed to float a moment – seemed even to turn his head in Travis's direction and grin – before slamming down on the ice, chest and stomach first, and barreling into the path of the speedster.

Nish swung his stick along the ice and clipped the puck off the stick of the little rusher. The River Rat tripped over Nish and crashed harmlessly into the far corner, the puck trickling in underneath him.

The River Rats were sure the referee had called a tripping penalty. Fans in the crowd cheered, and players on the bench rapped their sticks hard on the boards to signal their approval. But the referee had called no penalty. He had lost sight of the puck and blown the whistle, as he was supposed to.

The River Rats' coach was screaming for an explanation.

"The kid played the puck first," the referee told him. "Fair and square. And then your guy fell over him on the ice. No trip. Good play."

Now the Owls started rapping their sticks on the boards by the bench, an act that was instantly halted by Muck.

"We'll have none of that," he said. "This is a hockey game, not a theatrical performance."

When play resumed, Andy took the face-off and managed to slip the puck back between his skates to Nish. Nish looked down the ice, faked a pass up to Jesse, then took off himself.

Travis and Sarah were watching from the bench. "Let's not have the Mario move," Sarah said.

Nish was at center ice, still carrying the puck. He wasn't the fastest on the ice, but he had more determination than anyone. And when Nish decided to play, he could really play.

Up over the blue line and he still had the puck, though three Rats were trying to check him. He stopped suddenly, slipping the puck back just as one skater flew past, then tucked it between the skates of the defenseman ahead coming straight at him.

Nish had only one player to beat. He faked a quick shot and instead pushed the puck to the side, looping back in a curl toward the blue line, where the one remaining defender tried a poke check and fell.

He was in free.

"No Mario!" Sarah screamed from the bench.

No worries. Nish came in, faked the shot on net, forehand, backhand, and then back to front. The Rats' goaltender, trying to anticipate the shot, made the first move. The wrong move, it turned out.

Nish very gently tucked the puck into the open net and turned to skate back.

The River Rats and the crowd roared their disapproval. The Rats' coach was livid. "Fatso shoulda been in the box!" he screamed at the referee. Travis was glad Muck never screamed like that. Nor would Muck insult a player, no matter how upset he might be inside.

You could almost always predict what Muck might say or do. Nish, however, was not behaving like Nish. Where was the fist pump? Where was the slide on shin pads? Where was the leap into the air and the butt-check against the glass? ("Nish's Ovechkin," the kids called it.) Where was the race to the Owls' bench to punch gloves with his teammates and soak in the praise?

This was a new Nish. Crouched over, his stick across his shin pads, Bobby Orr style, Nish merely drifted back to his defense posting at center ice as if he'd just come off the bench.

Sarah and Travis turned to look at each other. There was nothing to say. Laughter was the only possible response.

The Owls won 4–2. Sarah scored on a rebound left behind by Dmitri on a nice rush, and in the dying seconds, Travis scored an empty netter – he thought of them as half-goals rather than real goals – when the Rats were trying to tie it up.

It had been a clean match, and the River Rats had proved to be good opponents.

Nish, the hero of the moment, dressed quietly, and for once carried his offensive underwear over to the laundry bag rather than tossing it without caring where it landed.

"What's up with you?" Sarah asked him. "Mr. Humility on the ice and now Mr. Helper in the dressing room?"

Nish grinned. "All part of the maturing process," he said. "I'm no longer in school, so I'm now a grown-up, right?"

No one bothered with an answer.

On the way back to the city center from the Wilmington rink, Mr. Dillinger pulled the team bus in at the first McDonald's golden-arches sign.

The Owls all cheered his decision. All except one.

Sam informed the team that she would not be going in with them.

"I no longer eat meat," she told them.

"I'll eat yours for you," Nish offered.

For once, Sam did not shoot him a reply. "I am a vegetarian now," she said very quietly.

"*Free the celery!*" Nish shouted.

So much for the "maturing process," thought Travis.

7

The scientific career of inventor Wayne Nishikawa was not off to a great start. Having quit school, like Ben Franklin, he was now determined to invent something – but unfortunately he had no idea what.

But then the small plastic disc shooter he had purchased at Mr. D's Stupid Stop gave him an idea, and Data, who was as close to a scientific genius as the Owls could claim, agreed to serve as Nish's assistant.

The disc launcher, Nish said, could be adapted to become an "automatic puck shooter." At Data's suggestion, he even laid out a "prospectus" for the invention, all dutifully written up by Data on his tablet computer:

The "Nishikawa Stinger" automatic puck shooter will do for the sport of hockey what the automatic pitcher has done for baseball and the automatic server has done for tennis. Coaches, hockey schools, and goaltenders will be able to dial up the types of shots they wish to face – slap shot, hoist, snap shot, saucer pass, bouncer – and choose the speed of shot, from "minor hockey" to "NHL." The "Nishikawa Stinger" will run off electricity and be entirely portable, for use everywhere from an NHL rink to an outdoor rink to a driveway. Cost to be determined.

Nish and Data – well, actually Data – were busy drawing up models on Data's tablet. Data was also compiling a list of materials necessary for them to build the first prototype of the machine.

Travis wondered exactly what Nish had done apart from lend his name to the ridiculous idea.

Travis was not the only one wondering about Nish. His teammates were still talking about Nish's lack of hotdogging after he had scored that spectacular goal against the River Rats.

And then, of course, there was Nish's mother.

In the evening after the game against the River Rats, Muck asked Nish to meet him in the lobby. When Nish went down, fully expecting to be congratulated for his mature behavior following his magnificent goal, he found the Screech Owls' coach sitting in a chair, rubbing his large hands together, and looking worried.

"Sit down, young man," Muck said seriously.

Nish sat, his own hands twisting with concern.

"I've received a call from your mother," Muck began. "She told me about the postcard you sent her. I am presuming that this was your idea of a little joke, correct?"

"No, sir. I meant it. I *mean* it. I'm going to quit school – just like Ben Franklin. I'm going to be a famous inventor."

"You do realize it's against the law to quit school until you're sixteen, don't you?"

"Ben Franklin was ten."

"Ben Franklin lived at a time when there was child labor. And people owned slaves. You don't live back then, Mr. Nishikawa. You live now, and you've upset your mother rather badly."

"She'll be proud of me when she sees what I've invented," Nish countered.

"And what's that?"

"A puck-shooting machine," Nish said proudly. "Me 'n' Data."

"Data and I."

"No, *me* 'n' Data! Not you 'n' Data."

"And you don't see why you still need to go to school?"

"No, why?"

Muck closed his eyes. He almost seemed to be giving up. But he had something to say and was determined to say it.

"I want you to listen to me, young man," he said to Nish. "And I want you to listen very closely."

Nish nodded.

"You know I played junior hockey, correct?" Nish nodded again. "I played with people who went on to the NHL. It was good hockey."

"You were lucky."

"No, son. I was unlucky first, and only after that I got lucky. I broke this leg here." Muck tapped his bad leg. "I broke it so badly I never played another game. I had no choice but to stick with school and try to make something of myself other than a hockey player. Other guys weren't so lucky. They didn't break their legs. Instead, hockey broke their hearts. Because they believed they would be playing in the National Hockey League, they dropped out of school the second they could. They had no need for school. They were hockey stars.

65

"And they were – up to a point. They were stars when they were young, and average players when they got older and the competition got harder – and soon enough they just weren't good enough. They didn't make pro. And then they found out they had nothing to fall back on. They were lucky to end up selling cars or delivering beer. They put all their eggs in the hockey basket, and their eggs broke. Do you understand what I'm saying?"

"You can't play hockey with eggs?"

"You're a great smart aleck, Mr. Nishikawa, but you aren't nearly as smart as you think you are. Now, I'm going to call your mother back and tell her you meant that card as a joke, okay? Are you good with that? Because that's what it is, young man – a joke. Do you hear me?"

Nish knew this was no time for fooling or playing dumb. And since that was all he usually did, he had trouble doing anything else. So he just nodded.

Muck nodded back, then stood up and walked away to make his phone call.

8

"NO FAIR!"

Nish was livid. He was bouncing around the hotel room, slamming his fist into furniture, slapping walls, and kicking beds and the coffee table. Beet red, near tears, flailing like a two-year-old having a tantrum at the mall. Yes, Travis thought to himself, Nish is all grown up and mature now.

"They can't do this to me!"

Data wheeled his chair out of the raging bull's way. Data had come to the door with his tablet, and Nish had thought they were going to work on the Nishikawa Stinger.

In a way, they were. Data had come to close the project down.

"I was looking through websites for propulsion ideas," Data told Nish, his fingers tapping on the tablet as he worked through a search engine. "And I'm afraid there already is a company out there that sells the same thing. It's called the Boni Goalie Trainer. Here, have a look."

Nish ripped the tablet from Data's hands and began poring over the website.

"*They stole my idea!*" he shouted.

Lars giggled. "I imagine they had the idea before yesterday, Nish."

"*No way!*" Nish yelled. "*Look at this.*" He practically slammed the screen into Lars's nose.

"They even stole my name," Nish hissed. "I called mine the Nishikawa Stinger. They have three pro models, and one of them is the Stinger! How do you explain that?"

Lars looked bewildered. "Maybe *coincidence*?"

"Ha!" said Nish. "I've just proved they stole

my idea. I should take them to court and sue the pants off them."

"I wouldn't recommend that," said Data, trying to bring Nish back to reality.

There was a light tap at the door and Travis hurried over to let whoever it was in.

It was Sarah, and she looked as white as a ghost.

"What's up?" asked Travis, instantly concerned.

"It's Sam," Sarah said in a shaky voice. "She's gone!"

9

"Sam picked up some leaflet at the demonstration outside the aquarium," Sarah said, as she and Travis hurried to the room Sam, Sarah, and Jenny were sharing. "She got really caught up in it."

"How do you mean?"

"Well, you saw her reaction at McDonald's. She says she's a vegan now."

"A *what*?"

"A vegan is like a vegetarian times a hundred. She says she'll never eat an animal product again – no beef, pork, chicken, seafood, not even milk or cheese."

"She'd die."

"No, she wouldn't. She'd eat vegetables and other foods – just nothing that has any connection to any living creature. She says her world was changed forever at that rally outside the aquarium."

"I thought they were a little extreme, didn't you? It looked to me like the penguins were happier and safer there than they would be in the wild."

"Doesn't matter what you and I might think, Trav – Sam has become a true believer. She must have found something in that leaflet that made her head out this evening on her own. She didn't tell any of us she was going. I tried to find the leaflet but she must have taken it with her."

"Wait!" Travis stopped fast and reached for his back pocket. "I might have it right here."

He fished in his pocket and pulled out the leaflet. He hadn't even looked at it when he took it, and had forgotten all about it until now.

Quickly he unfolded the leaflet. "FREE THE PENGUINS!" was written in bold letters across the top. Inside was a lot of information on human cruelty to animals around the world, including photos of tightly penned pigs and beakless chickens and force-fed geese, and several of wild animals struggling to escape from traps. One showed a fox that had chewed its own foot off to get free of a snare.

"Yuck!" said Travis, and he quickly turned the page. He and Sarah scanned the words as quickly as they could in search of a clue, any clue, to where Sam might have gone.

On the back page, they found it. An announcement with a green box around it:

INFORMATION SESSION
Boston's "FREE THE PENGUINS!" cell
will hold an information session
Tuesday evening at Boston Public Garden
by the Swan Boat pond.
All welcome!
Donate what you can to the movement.
Session begins at 7:00 p.m.

"I bet she's there," Sarah said.
"Boston Public Garden isn't far."

"Let's go!"

"Shouldn't we tell someone?" asked Travis, ever cautious.

Sarah shook her head. "Sam might get in trouble for sneaking off. Let's just go ourselves and see what she's doing."

10

The evening sun was casting long shadows across the Common as Sarah and Travis made their way toward the Boston Public Garden. The big trees along the Swan Boat pond loomed like dark giants in the shadows.

On the bridge above the docks, where tourists were lining up for the final Swan Boat tours of the day, a group of people was gathered. They were listening intently to a woman who was talking without a microphone but loudly enough to be heard even across the water, where Sarah and Travis were hurrying along the shoreline trail.

As they hurried, they picked up snippets, the loud voice fading in and out in the wind and the trees.

"The Second American Revolution should be about the rights of animals . . . !

"Drastic situations call for drastic measures . . .

"I would lay down my life to save an innocent creature in captivity . . ."

By the time Travis and Sarah arrived at the bridge, the meeting was already breaking up. Some of the protesters were cheering and shouting slogans and brandishing placards like the ones the Owls had seen earlier.

They looked frantically about for Sam. Several young people were there, but they all appeared to be with their parents. Travis and Sarah couldn't see Sam anywhere.

They stood in the center of the bridge, turning both ways, uncertain what to do. People were leaving from both ends of the bridge and going in all directions.

"I'll go this way," Travis suggested. "You go that way. Meet back here in fifteen minutes."

Sarah nodded and took off in pursuit of a group of protesters making their way toward the Common. Travis ran back in the direction they had come from, hurrying along the shoreline trail, checking group after group.

He had soon passed all the people who'd come this way. No sign of Sam. He doubled back, checking as many people again as he could, but he quickly realized that unless the protesters were still carrying their placards, he could no longer tell them from all the other people out walking around.

He hoped Sarah was having better luck.

But Sarah was not. She had skirted the ticket booth for the Swan Boat rides and hurried along to the street, checking everywhere for her friend. She crossed at the lights and went into Boston Common, but too many paths were branching every which way. After a short while spent running frantically across the large park, she, too, realized it was hopeless. She turned back toward the bridge.

Sarah was exhausted by the time she got back near the bridge. She stopped and tried to catch her breath, hoping the stitch in her side would soon go. Ahead of her, already on the bridge, she spotted Travis.

He was waving for her to join him. He looked worried.

Sarah was still gulping air when she reached him. Travis signaled for her to say nothing and pointed over to a spot across the water from the docks. There, under a very large elm tree, was Sam. She was deep in conversation with the woman who had been talking to the protesters.

"I'm pretty sure that's the woman who was wearing the penguin suit," said Travis. "Sounded like her, too."

Sarah nodded, still short of breath. She had thought the same thing.

"What's that on her neck?" Sarah said, squinting.

Travis had seen it, too. A dark patch. "Looks like a tattoo," he said, "but I can't make it out."

The woman – dressed entirely in black, and tall and lean as a scarecrow – was facing Sam, with a hand on each of Sam's shoulders and her head leaned in low toward her. She was talking very intently to Sam, and Sam was nodding quickly, as if in agreement with every word the woman was saying.

Suddenly the woman hugged Sam. Sam hugged her back, hard, and the two of them broke apart. Hand in hand, they began walking back toward the bridge.

Sarah had her breath back, and she couldn't stop herself from calling out.

"Sam! Up here!"

Sam looked up, startled to see Sarah and Travis looking down at her and waving. She hesitated, then waved back.

The woman looked up, eyes blazing on either side of a hawk-like nose. She did not seem pleased.

Sarah and Travis hurried down off the bridge to meet Sam and her new friend. Sam had turned rather pink. She certainly hadn't expected to see them.

"We were worried about you!" Sarah said, giving Sam a big hug. "You never said where you were going."

"I just slipped out for a bit," said Sam a bit nervously. "I was just heading back."

"We'll go with you," said Travis.

"And who do we have here?" the woman asked. Her voice sounded like someone acting. Travis looked at her. Her mouth was smiling, but not her eyes.

Sam sputtered introductions. "Sarah and Travis, this is Frances Assisi."

"Nice to meet you," the woman said. "Sam here might be the brightest young woman I have ever met. She understands the cause."

Travis couldn't keep from wincing. The *cause*? What sort of talk was that?

Sarah's face remained expressionless. "What cause?" she asked.

The woman gave a dismissive little laugh. "The great fight for animal rights," she said, as if it were obvious.

"I'm against the aquarium," Sam suddenly stated.

"Why?" said Sarah. "You liked it well enough yesterday. You had a good time. We all did."

"She didn't understand then," said the woman. Sam just nodded in agreement. "Samantha knows now that we humans have no right to imprison animals. Many people in this country are against the death penalty, yet we carry it out every day on innocent cattle and pigs and chickens. We are destroying our oceans by dragging nets that scoop up every living creature, and we kill and throw away the ones that are caught accidentally. We humans are the single most destructive force the world has ever known. We are killers, until we decide, as Sam has decided, to stop the killing — isn't that right, Samantha?"

Sam seemed embarrassed. "Y-yes," she said.

Frances smiled the same emotionless smile as before, her eyes all the while looking at them sharply. Travis felt as if he were being scanned with a laser. There was something so strangely intense about her stare that he could not bear it.

When Frances looked back at Sam, they could see the dark mark on her neck. It was, as Travis had guessed, a tattoo. A penguin in flight.

Travis's first reaction was to note that penguins

couldn't fly. He wondered if the woman really didn't know that. But then he got the message: *freedom*. A penguin flying away.

"We'd better get back before Muck and Mr. D find you're missing," he said to Sam.

Sam nodded.

"We'll take her back," Sarah said firmly to the woman. She quickly took Sam's free hand and pulled her, just enough that the woman's grip on Sam loosened.

"I guess," said Sam.

"Stay in touch," Frances said. She raised her right hand to show another tattoo – a blurred mark in the center of her palm.

11

"You're sure that's the name?" Data asked.

"Pretty sure," said Travis. "Frances A-see-see, or something like that. She didn't spell it out for us."

Data had been fiddling with his tablet. He was supposed to be looking for a new invention for Nish, but Travis had interrupted his research.

Later in the morning, the Owls would be heading for the rink and Game 3 of the Paul Revere Peewee Invitational, but right now Travis wanted to know what was up with this strange woman who seemed to have put a spell on Sam.

Data was taking quite a long time, his fingers dancing as he jumped from one website to the next.

"Very, very strange," Data finally said.

"What? What have you found?"

"There are a couple of news stories here concerning a 'Frances Assisi,' who was arrested for throwing paint over fur coats at a fashion show."

Data began reading. "Isobel Twining, a.k.a. Frances Assisi, forty-three, was detained and later released by Boston police . . .'"

"What's a.k.a.?"

Data looked at Travis as if he couldn't believe he wouldn't know. "It means 'also known as.' It means Frances Assisi isn't her real name – she's really Isobel Twining."

"Why would she do that?" Travis asked. "Such a strange name."

Data's fingers moved over the tablet and a new website popped up.

"I think this is your answer," he said, spinning the tablet so Travis could see.

It was an encyclopedia entry on St. Francis of Assisi. St. Francis was born in 1181 or 1182 and died in 1226 – *nearly 800 years ago*. He was Italian, and his real name was Giovanni di Pietro di Bernardone. His "a.k.a.," Travis noted, was Francesco, or Francis – and Data pointed out that "Frances," with an *e*, was the feminine version of the name. St. Francis had been a Catholic preacher and was renowned for his love of all creatures. A couple of years after his death he was named a saint and was still known as the patron saint of animals.

Travis nodded. Now he understood.

He read more on the patron saint of animals. He found that the real Francis Assisi claimed to have seen visions and was the first person known to have the signs of the crucifixion appear on his hands and feet – signs taken at the time to be nothing short of a holy miracle.

So, Travis thought, that would explain the tattoo in the palm of the woman's hand. He didn't need to see the other palm or her feet to know what he might find there. This was getting really weird.

"Do you think she's crazy?" Travis asked Data.

"I have no idea," said Data. "You met her, not me. But obviously Sam doesn't think she's crazy. And they aren't the only two people in the world who believe you shouldn't eat animals. There are millions who hold that view. So it's pretty hard to call her crazy based on a fake name."

Travis couldn't argue with Data's logic.

"Don't you have a game to get ready for?" Data asked.

Travis snapped out of his confused thoughts. A game, yes, they had a game to play. That's why the Screech Owls were in Boston, after all.

"Thanks for this," Travis said. "See you at the rink."

"Get your head back in the game, too," Data said. "Okay?"

Travis nodded. "I will."

12

I t turned out to be easier said than done. Travis had his head back on hockey – he thought. He had checked the schedule. The Owls would be up against the Detroit Wheels, another peewee team they had previously met, and beaten. But only barely. The two teams had met at the Big Apple International in New York City, and the Owls had won 6–5 in the opener and then 5–4 in overtime for the championship. Nish had been the hero in both games, and naturally he would want to be the hero again today in Boston.

As they got their equipment together for the bus out to Wilmington, Travis and Nish talked about the previous games against the Wheels. Nish had been going on and on about the spectacular goal that had won the championship. He had tried a move made famous years earlier by Hall of Famer Pavel Bure. Nish had carried the puck up ice and ended up back of the Wheels' net. From there, he had flipped the puck high into the air, over the goal and the Detroit goaltender, then slipped out around front to take his own pass and rip a shot past the goalie for the winning point.

From the way Nish told it, he'd been the only Owl on the ice against six hundred Detroit Wheels and had single-handedly won the game. He was conveniently forgetting the Owls' four other goals, which had taken them into overtime. But what could Travis expect from his goofy buddy? Nish was never going to change. He claimed he'd matured since "quitting" school, but Travis couldn't see it.

Nish was still boasting when Mr. D came up the steps of the bus, closed the door, and stepped to the front of the aisle with a quick announcement.

"We're going to be short a player this afternoon, boys and girls. Sam isn't feeling well and will stay back in her room. So let's win one for her, okay?"

Several of the Owls shouted back.

"Okay!"

"This one's for Sam!"

But not Travis Lindsay. He spun in his seat away from Nish the Braggart and looked for Sarah. He found her back a few seats on the other side of the aisle.

Sarah shrugged and held up her hands.

She had no answer for him.

The Detroit Wheels were every bit the team they had been in New York: fast, smart, well-coached, strong, and determined. But the Owls were no longer the Owls who had arrived in Boston with their "hockey muscles" weak and their timing as off as a broken clock.

Travis felt right from the moment he stepped onto the fresh ice, his newly sharpened skates – thank you, Mr. D! – cutting in hard as he sizzled through the first corner. He skipped a puck off the crossbar on his second try. He felt good and strong and fast.

Sarah was also rounding into game shape. She won the opening face-off by plucking the puck out of midair, and with a backhand slap she sent it instantly up ice, where Dmitri picked it up and flew in fast. Forehand, backhand, puck high into the roof of the net. The Owls were up 1–0 and the game had barely started.

Soon, however, it was apparent that the Owls could have used Sam back on defense. The Wheels' coaching staff had realized that, without Sam's speed and smarts, the Owls were weak on that side, and their players kept using the advantage to hound less-skilled defensemen like Fahd to cough up the puck. If either Nish or Lars wasn't there, the Owls were in trouble.

The Wheels tied the game at 1–1 on a deflection, then went ahead 2–1 just before the period ended, when Jenny misplayed a long shot that bounced twice and changed direction.

Midway through the second, with the score tied 2–2, after a nifty bit of stickhandling by Derek, Nish sent a long pass that bounced off the boards and slid fast down the ice between a hard-skating Travis and Dmitri.

Dmitri used his skate blade to kick the puck up to his stick. But the Detroit goaltender was ready for him this time. He read Dmitri's forehand-backhand fake perfectly this time and had the near side sealed off when Dmitri was ready to shoot.

Dmitri was also ready, however. He had played it the same way on purpose to pull the goaltender as tight to the post as possible. Instead of shooting, Dmitri sent a quick, short pass to Travis, who popped the puck into the net. The Owls had the lead again.

But the Wheels were not to be so easily beaten. Their top center scored on a booming slap shot early in the third, and with only a minute to go, a shot from the point ricocheted in past Jenny to give the Wheels a 4–3 lead.

Muck sent Lars and Nish out together. All game he had split them up to help cover for the loss of Sam, but now he needed his best on the ice if the Owls were to have a chance.

He sent out Sarah's line. And then, once Lars had dumped the puck up over center and into the Wheels' end, he called Jenny off for the extra attacker, sending out Derek.

It was a gut call by Muck. Mr. D's son wouldn't usually be the choice as an extra attacker, but he had played probably his best game of the year. Muck was playing a hunch. And Muck's hunches had a way of working out.

Nish and Lars worked a give-and-go up the ice, and Lars fired a puck in around the boards. Travis, anticipating the dump-in, hurried along tight to the left boards. Instead of taking the puck on his stick as it rounded the boards, he let it tick off his skate blade out to the top of the left circle, where Derek was waiting.

Derek one-timed a hard shot. The Detroit goaltender brilliantly kicked it out with his left pad, but the puck landed right on the stick of Lars, who lofted it over the fallen goaltender into the Detroit net.

Detroit Wheels 4, Screech Owls 4.

"This is *my* time to shine!" Nish hissed at Travis as the horn blew to call an end to regulation time. There was nothing in the world Nish liked better than overtime hockey – providing he could be the hero.

But it was not to be. Two minutes into over-time, Nish took a penalty for tripping, and no amount of whining to the referee could take it away.

The Wheels had the power play they needed. Soon they had the Owls boxed in down at their own end as they worked the puck around the edges in search of a clear shot on Jenny.

They set the shot up perfectly – or almost per-fectly – as their top defenseman found himself in the slot and ready to hammer a one-timer.

Fahd, put out by Muck out of necessity, because Nish was unavailable, appeared out of nowhere, sliding and spinning toward the puck as the big defenseman continued through on his swing.

He slapped the puck. It flew off his stick blade – straight into Fahd's shin pads.

The puck hit Fahd's pads so hard it rebounded, still in the air, all the way back to center ice, where, of all people, Simon Milliken picked it up, raced in, and shot.

Or, rather, he missed his shot. Simon's stick slid over top of the puck and it barely changed direction.

It was almost nothing, but it was enough to fool the Detroit Wheels' goaltender. The goalie watched helplessly from the far side of his net – where he'd leaped in anticipation of Simon's shot – as the puck moved, slowly as a curling rock, just over the red line.

Victory for the Screech Owls, 5–4 in overtime!

The Owls flooded off the bench and over the boards. Dmitri raced first to Simon, leaping and landing on him and crashing the surprised little forward into the boards past the despondent Detroit goaltender.

Sarah raced for Fahd, who had made it all possible, hugging him and slapping his pads. Fahd seemed to wonder what it was he had done to deserve all the attention.

The penalty box door opened and out skated a red-faced, scowling Wayne Nishikawa, looking for all the world like his team had just suffered its worst defeat in history.

Travis took note. What was it about Nish that Travis liked anyway? At the moment, he couldn't be sure.

"Good game," Muck told them in the dressing room. "We're in the final now. We just don't know yet who we'll play. There are three possibilities – these guys we just played, the Young Blackhawks, or the Mini-Penguins from Pittsburgh. Could be any of them. We don't care."

And with that, the coach stepped out of the dressing room, leaving the Owls to undress and talk amongst themselves.

"You *rule*, Fahd!" Sarah said. "And you, Simon! You're our first two stars."

"Hey," protested Nish. "Who's the guy who sent the pass down the ice that got us into overtime?"

Sarah feigned ignorance. "I have no idea, Nish – who would that be?"

He answered with a raspberry.

13

I t was morning. The summer sun streamed warm through the hotel room window as Travis sat on the edge of his bed and rubbed the sleep out of his eyes with the backs of his fists.

There was a light knock at the door. The others were still sleeping – Nish snoring like Travis's grandfather did when he napped at the cottage – and Travis opened the door quietly.

It was Sarah. Sam was gone again.

"When?" Travis asked.

"No idea," Sarah said. "I thought she was in the next bed, but she'd just covered up a couple of pillows to make it look like she was."

"Does Muck know? Or Mr. D?"

Sarah shook her head.

Travis felt the pincers of a dilemma begin to squeeze his brain. He was captain of the Screech Owls. He had a duty to look out for his teammates. But he also had a duty to the coach and general manager of the team. If he went to Muck and Mr. D, Sam might get in trouble – and for all he knew, she might simply be down in the lobby. If he and Sarah found her there, their worries would have been for nothing. Then again, they had reason to be worried. Sam was not acting herself.

A quick check might be the right thing to do.

"Wait there," Travis said. "I'll get dressed and be right with you."

Nish stirred as Travis dressed. His snoring stopped, then started up again even more loudly. The others were sound asleep.

Travis slipped out the door and closed it gently. "We'll check the lobby first," he said to Sarah.

They quickly caught an elevator and descended to the lobby without a stop. It was still very early in the morning. They searched everywhere, but to no avail.

Travis hurried to the revolving doors on the side of the hotel nearest the New England Aquarium, Sarah moving quickly to catch up to him. There were few people out and about so early. One hotel worker was watering plants, and another was washing down the sidewalks with a hose.

"Over there!" Sarah said, pointing toward the aquarium.

Travis turned and looked. On the side of the aquarium closest to the harbor, he saw the yellow caution tape and barricades to keep people back from the construction work, but there was no one at the site. A large black tarp completely covered the gap in the concrete that the crew had opened up on the aquarium wall.

Off to one side, taking photographs of the construction site, was Frances Assisi, a.k.a. Isobel Twining.

Sam was there as well.

Travis and Sarah looked at each other. Travis grimaced; Sarah looked perplexed. What was Sam up to?

They wandered over. "Frances" noticed them before Sam did, and scowled. She obviously had no desire to be disturbed.

"Sam!" Sarah called out.

Sam turned, blushing deeply, as if caught doing something she'd been warned not to.

"Hey, Sarah, Trav . . . what's up?"

"We were wondering the same," said Travis.

Sam swallowed. "I couldn't sleep. Still not feeling well, I guess . . . so I came out for some air, and Frances was out here, so I just started helping her."

Frances was smiling at them now – the same emotionless smile – and moved in quickly. "I'm a professional photographer as well as my other work," she said. "Sam's been helping me take photos of the aquarium for an article I'm working on. They won't let me take any photos inside."

I'm not surprised, Travis thought to himself. This woman had *trouble* written all over her.

"And we've been talking about animal rights, haven't we, Sam?" Frances went on.

"Right," said Sam.

"Sam's going to start up a youth wing of our little group once she gets home, isn't that right, Sam?"

Sam nodded. "Frances sees this movement spreading by the power of kids just like us," she said. "We refuse to eat animals, and our parents have no choice but to stop killing them. It would be the ultimate grassroots movement – one we think could take off to include the whole world."

Travis and Sam both looked at their friend, blinking. Neither said anything, but each knew what the other was thinking: this didn't sound like Sam. She was using Frances's words. It was almost like she was under some weird spell.

Frances began taking pictures of other parts of the aquarium and the boardwalk, but she was doing so without much enthusiasm.

Travis looked back at the construction site. When Frances had been taking photographs of it, she had been working carefully, deliberately.

She appeared to know exactly what she was looking for. Now it seemed she was just taking shots at random.

Travis didn't believe that Frances was working on any "article."

"Muck's going to be looking for us," said Sarah. Sam nodded.

"We'd better get back," added Travis.

"B-bye," Sam said to Frances, as if she were being dragged away.

"Keep in touch, Sam," Frances said, the mouth smiling again. "We have a world to change."

It was still early enough, when the three Screech Owls returned to the lobby, that none of their teammates had come down from their rooms yet. Muck was sitting in a chair in one corner, reading the Boston newspapers, and didn't notice them come in through the revolving doors. Travis pulled Sam's arm, leading her off to the opposite corner, where the three teammates could talk alone.

"What's up with you?" Travis asked. He tried not to sound too angry – or too much like their vice-principal at Tamarack Public School – but he knew he sounded cranky and annoyed.

"Nothing," Sam answered, as if she didn't quite understand why Travis would ask such a question.

"You've been acting *weird*," said Sarah, looking genuinely concerned.

"Weird?" Sam said. "*I'm* the one that's weird, while you eat innocent animals that have no idea what real grass or blue sky looks like? *I'm* the weirdo, when the rest of the world thinks it's a wonderful thing to steal creatures from their mothers and their natural homes and put them on display in zoos and aquariums so humans can pay money and gawk at them? *I'm* the weird one? Give me a break!"

"Man," said Travis, "that woman sure has got to you, hasn't she?"

"That *woman*," answered Sam, "is right. Frances has a lot of followers, people who believe in her and what she is doing."

"And you're one of them?" asked Sarah.

"Yes. She's going to change the world, and I plan to help her."

"How can you do that?" said Travis. "Humans have eaten meat since we all lived in caves. And places like the aquarium do good work – they *save* animals!"

"All that's just public relations," Sam snorted. "They do that to convince people everything else they do is good. Is it good to take penguins and fish away from their homes and family?"

"Fish don't really have 'family,'" Sarah said.

"How do you know? How does anyone know how a fish feels? Or a turtle? Or that little penguin that was fooled into thinking I was its mother? You saw how it cried and ran after me. I could have done anything I wanted to it, including chopping its head off and eating it."

"But you didn't," said Travis. "You wouldn't."

"So? What's the difference between that penguin and a little goose that's trapped in a cage so it can't move and is force-fed so that its liver swells up like a balloon just so you can have something to spread on a cracker? Is *that* fair?"

Travis and Sarah did not know what to say. Sam had a point, thought Travis, but if you agreed about not harming a single living thing, wouldn't that mean you couldn't eat vegetables and fruit? What were humans to do for food? *Suck on a stone?* If you took anything to extremes, it rarely made sense.

Travis decided to change his approach.

"You can't change the world by holding up a bunch of signs."

"You have to begin somewhere," Sam said. "If people didn't fight back against wrongs, we'd still have slaves."

Travis couldn't argue with that. He thought of the little grave marker – "Frank" – and how profoundly it had seemed to affect Wilson.

"It took a war to put an end to that," Sam added.

"But that's *people*," Sarah protested. "No one is going to go to war for animal rights."

"Frances is," Sam said. "She declared war against furs – and now she's declaring war against animals in captivity."

"She has no army," Travis said before he could stop himself. He regretted it even as he said it.

"Who says?"

"That little group of protesters?" Travis asked. "What can they do?"

Sam sniffed and turned her back on them.

"You might be surprised," she snapped.

14

"*What the . . . !*"

First had come the sound of Nish yanking open the big zipper on his equipment bag. There was no other noise in the dressing room. Under strict orders from Andy and Jenny, who were clearly the ringleaders in this attack on Nish's stinking bag, all the other Screech Owls had "zipped" their own mouths shut.

"You've got to be kidding!" Nish moaned, his big face pinched beet red.

Mr. Dillinger snorted from the back of the room, where he was busy unpacking his skate-sharpening machine. Mr. D had been in on the joke from the moment he let Andy and Jenny have access to the big bag with number 44 stitched on the side.

"*This is way, way, WAY over the top!*" Nish screamed, his eyes so tightly shut it seemed they would leak blood.

No one said a word. The rest of the Owls shook with suppressed laughter. Nish looked around helplessly, then dumped the contents of his bag all over the dressing room floor.

"*Disgusting!*" he snorted.

The laughter burst like a dam. The Owls roared their approval as deodorant sticks and air freshener sprays tumbled out of Nish's hockey bag along with his usual equpment, followed by some lovely pink material that fluttered and fell like autumn leaves on top of the pile.

Women's underwear.

Nish's beet-red face turned even redder as he fought for the words he needed to lash back at his teammates. When he could find none, he asked the obvious.

"Where's my hockey underwear?"

"We 'disposed' of it," Sam said.

"We bought you new stuff," Fahd giggled. "Nice-smelling stuff – have a whiff – you won't believe the difference."

"Are you some sort of sicko?" Nish asked. "I want my own gauchies back!"

Sarah reached into her own equipment bag and drew out a plastic garbage bag tied at the top. She threw it at Nish, who caught it in the air.

"Here's your stupid gauchies," Sarah said. "Sam and I took the liberty of washing them at the hotel."

"Washed them twice!" Sam added.

Nish tore open the garbage bag. His clean underwear, nicely folded by Sarah, tumbled onto the floor. He picked up his long johns and smelled them.

"I can't play in these," he said. "They don't smell like me. They smell like somebody's stupid garden!"

"Then your only other choice is these," Sam said, using her stick blade to pluck up some frilly pink underwear from Nish's jumble of equipment. She raised them up toward Nish, who promptly swatted them away, to the howls of the rest of the team.

"Or maybe you could *invent* some hockey underwear that doesn't stink like a skunk rolled in horse manure!" Lars shouted.

"Yeah!" declared Andy. "Gauchies with built-in air fresheners like you have in a car!"

"Throwaway gauchies!" shrieked Jenny. "Or underwear that *dissolves* on you right after you've played!"

The Owls groaned as one. The image of Nish, standing in the dressing room after a game, his underwear slowly dissolving, was just too much to bear.

"Gross!" said Jesse.

"Disgusting!" said Fahd.

"*I'm gonna hurl!*" Simon Milliken shouted.

The Owls all laughed while Nish kicked at his equipment, as if somehow he could boot the underwear all the way back to whatever store his teammates had purchased it at.

The giggles stopped quickly when the dressing room door opened and Muck walked in, closing the door quietly behind him. The coach had his game face on.

"Mr. D and I scouted these Mini-Penguins at their last game," Muck told them. "And they are good. Not just good, but extremely good. They play in some Pittsburgh program that has ice all year long. So just like that Chicago team you met in Game One, they're in mid-season form. You should bear that in mind."

Muck looked around. He stared hard at Nish, then looked down briefly at the floor in front of him. Nish was trying to cover up the frilly underwear with his feet. Muck stared hard at Nish again until the embarrassed Screech Owl was forced to look back and hold Muck's stare.

"Mr. Nishikawa," Muck said.

"Yes," Nish answered.

"No glory plays, okay? We need you back there at all times."

Nish nodded.

"Get dressed," Muck told them all.

The coach paused, a grin flickering at the side of his mouth. He looked down at Nish's feet a second time.

"Just make sure you put on your own stuff, everybody. Okay?"

The Owls all giggled as Muck pulled the door closed behind him. Nish was burning red. He kicked hard at the unwanted underwear.

Travis felt it was time to be captain. "Get ready," he announced. "Time to put on our game faces."

Sam couldn't resist. "Care to borrow my lipstick, Mr. Nishikawa?"

15

Penguins, Travis thought. What a strange name for a hockey team. Slow birds that couldn't fly . . .

Warm-up was just over. He had hit the crossbar on his third attempt – not the best start, but at least he had done it – and the two teams were getting ready for the puck drop.

These penguins were not small and cute and cuddly like the birds at the aquarium. The Mini-Penguins were big and fast, and even during warm-up they had seemed mean, as if just waiting to go after the best Owls, which of course meant Travis's line with Sarah and Dmitri.

Team names were funny. There had once been the Mighty Ducks, named after a movie. And what was even mildly threatening about a team called the Maple Leafs? There had been all that controversy about teams using names like the Cleveland Indians, the Washington Redskins, and the Kansas City Chiefs – even the Chicago Blackhawks – in hockey. And then there were crazy names, like the Maniacs and the Devils.

What about the Screech Owls? Travis wondered. Where had Muck come up with that one? And yet Travis and every other player on the team wore the Owls logo with pride. If you lived in Tamarack, it was the team you dreamed of playing for. So it must be a good name.

The Mini-Penguins played more like hawks, or eagles – swooping down ice fast and fearless, always dangerous whenever they had the puck on a rush.

Travis could see why Muck had ordered Nish to keep back and stay away from glory plays. The

Owls needed their defense to be solid. They couldn't take any chances.

The Penguins had one particularly gifted player. To Travis, he seemed like Mario Lemieux and Sidney Crosby rolled into one. He was tall, with a tremendous reach, which meant he could hold on to the puck like Lemieux; but he was also powerful and could twist and turn in the corners like Crosby.

The big kid soon had the Penguins up 2–0, and the opening period was still far from over. Every time Travis's line came out, the big kid's line was also out. The two coaches were clearly matching lines. Best against best.

Travis knew his job would be to stay back and help out the defense whenever needed. He would trail any rushes by Dmitri or Sarah and always be prepared to turn on a dime if the Penguins broke up an Owls rush and sent the puck back the other way. Twice already, Travis had been able to help out, once lifting the big Penguin's stick just before he could shoot, and once intercepting a pass from the same guy that would have given the Penguin's winger a sure goal.

Travis knew he was playing well. He knew from what he saw on the ice but also from a brief moment on the bench. He had felt Muck's big hand on the back of his neck, just above the throat protector. One quick squeeze and the hand was gone. Muck's way of saying "Well done."

With time running out in the opening period, Sarah picked up the puck in the Owls' end and darted straight up center. Travis was right with her, but still aware that he might be needed back if the puck turned over.

Dmitri was breaking ahead of her. Sarah flipped a pass high over the outstretched stick of a backpedaling defender, and Dmitri caught the puck in his glove and threw it down onto his stick. He was in free.

Sarah moved fast in case there was a rebound. Travis still held back. Dmitri moved in, went to his classic play – forehand fake, backhand high to the roof of the net – but the Penguins' goaltender got his left shoulder up and blocked it.

The puck flipped through the air like a horse-shoe, coming to rest right on Travis's stick. He fired hard and turned back, expecting the goaltender to kick out the rebound.

But the puck squeezed right through the sliding goalie's pads and into the net.

Travis was having a great game.

At the face-off, just before the puck dropped, the big Penguins' center looked hard at Travis. Travis couldn't be certain, but behind the player's face shield he could swear he saw a quick smile and a nod.

It felt as good as Muck's hand squeezing the back of his neck.

Late in the third period, with the game tied at 3–3, Lars and Jesse having added goals for the Owls, Nish wiggled over on the bench until he was beside Travis's forward line.

Nish's face was red and covered in sweat. Travis knew his friend was in full Nish game mode. He was playing his heart out, and he was listening to instructions from Muck and staying back.

Nish was breathing hard, gulping for air from his last shift, but he had something to say.

"Hail Mary," Nish hissed at Travis.

Travis nodded. He understood at once. The crazy Doug Flutie desperation pass that had won the football game for Boston College so long ago. Nish was going to send the puck high and deep, and he expected Travis to catch it.

Sarah leaped over the boards as Andy came off on the fly. Travis jumped onto the ice as soon as Derek reached the bench. Dmitri replaced Jesse on the far wing.

The big Penguins' center was circling his own net with the puck, readying for a rush up ice. Sarah moved in to check him, but he deftly turned back, using the net as a shield, and came up the far side. A nice bit of stickhandling, and he was through Dmitri and coming up hard over center.

Travis could see Nish skating backward fast, trying to cut off any lane the big center might use to set a winger free on a breakaway. He knew he'd have to cover for Nish if Nish overcommitted.

Travis dug deep and came back hard. But Nish had read the play perfectly. The big center was hoping to draw Fahd and Nish, the Owls' defense, his way and then loop a pass across ice to his right winger, coming fast down Travis's side.

The center sent a perfect saucer pass when he saw Nish moving to cut off the lane. The puck flew high over the outstretched sticks of Fahd and Nish and landed flat, with a slap, in the center of the ice.

Travis had anticipated the play. He gobbled up the puck before the winger could get it and turned hard back up ice.

But the big winger had seen Travis snare the pass and was now bearing down on him. Travis had two options: he could dump the puck out, delivering it right back to the Penguins, or he could drop it back.

Nish was well back, according to Muck's instructions, and Travis sent him a backhand pass off the boards. Nish got the puck as he moved behind Jeremy and the Owls' net.

Travis knew what to do. It was Hail Mary time. He took off as fast as he could skate.

As Travis crossed the blue line, Nish looked up and fired the puck as high and hard as he could.

Travis sensed the puck sailing past his head as he cleared center ice. It was just barely ahead of him. The puck dropped, skipped twice on the ice, and he was on it.

Breakaway!

Travis corralled the puck on the blade of his stick, making sure it settled flat. He was well ahead of the Penguins' defense.

Travis knew he was alone. No one to pass to. No one to grab a rebound. He had to score on his own.

As he came down, slightly on his off wing, Dmitri's patented play popped into his head.

The goalie was in position, barely wiggling as he moved deeper into his net as Travis came closer.

Forehand fake, backhand high. The puck pinged in off the crossbar.

Goal!

Screech Owls 4, Pittsburgh Mini-Penguins 3.

Travis could not have been happier. He'd been chosen player of the game for the Owls, while the big center had, naturally, been named player of the game for the Penguins. Thanks to the public address announcement, Travis now knew his name: Alex Schultz. They had both been given tiny medals, and as they skated back to their teammates, who were lined up on opposite blue lines, Schultz used his long reach to tap Travis on the shin pads.

Travis was smiling as he skated back, and the Owls all came out to tap his gloves or rap their sticks off his pads and pants.

All except Nish, who hung back.

Travis continued down the line of Owls until he reached Nish, who reluctantly fisted Travis's glove. Travis could almost see steam coming out of Nish's ears.

"It was *my* pass," Nish hissed. "*My* Hail Mary that won the game!"

Travis accepted the tap of the glove from his friend, but said nothing.

What could he possibly say?

16

Travis barely heard the tap on the door. He thought he was dreaming. Then it came again, a light tap, scarcely there, but a tap all the same.

He sat up in his bed. It was dark. Nish was breathing hard in the bed opposite, out like a light. The others were all still asleep.

The tap again.

He went to the door and pulled it open quietly, thinking there was likely no one there.

But there was. It was Sarah. And behind her was Sam.

Sam was in tears.

The three Screech Owls sat on the steps in the stairwell at the end of the corridor. It was unlikely anyone would come upon them there. Sam had stopped crying, but she was shaking. Strange, thought Travis: it was much warmer in the stairwell than it was in the air-conditioned rooms and corridors. Sarah had her arm around Sam and was rubbing her shoulder in an effort to comfort her.

Sam slowly got herself together, then began talking.

"Frances put me on her mobile contact list," she said. "The one she said was for her 'inner circle' only – the people she trusted. Ever since she had that trouble with the police over the fur, she's been convinced they were tracking her calls and e-mails.

So this was a special thing she was using that meant messages stayed private. They went direct and not through any server."

"I know about that," Travis said. "It's called pinning — my dad sometimes uses it when he's about to close a business deal."

"Anyway," said Sam. "She set up my phone so I could get those messages once I got home. I was going to start up a group there. But when I went to bed tonight, I started getting all these strange texts from her phone. I'm not sure they were meant for me, and I'm not sure what they mean."

Sam held out her phone so Travis could scroll through the text messages.

Travis read them out loud, then read them all again to himself. He had no idea what they meant.

"Free the Penguins!"

"Meet 9 a.m. sharp, you know where."

"Arrangements complete — it's a go, people!"

"Alarm set."

"St. Francis and St. Michael will guide us!"

"Census Day = Judgment Day."

"The last one scares me," said Sam. "Census Day equals Judgment Day."

"What's it mean?" asked Travis.

Sam took a deep breath. It was almost as if she didn't want to say what she thought. But she knew she had to. Her voice broke as she tried to explain.

"Well," she said. "Remember when we visited the aquarium, and Fahd asked how many creatures they had?"

"Yeah, sure," said Travis. "The guide said six hundred."

"Well, they said they didn't know for sure, but each year, they do a census, a count – and this week, they said, was when they'd be doing it."

"But what about Judgment Day?" Sarah asked. "And what's all that talk about saints?"

Sam swallowed. "Remember what Data told us about that St. Francis of Assisi? How he devoted his life to saving animals?"

"A bit," said Travis. "But who's St. Michael?"

"I googled that," said Sam. "Michael is the saint who's supposed to weigh the souls on Judgment Day and decide who was good and who was evil.

St. Francis was devoted to him and asked his followers to pray to St. Michael so they'd be ready for Judgment Day."

"Sounds weird," Travis said.

"Not to lots of people," said Sarah. "My grandmother has a calendar with all the saints' days marked."

"But *this* is weird," said Travis. "Put it all together. We know about her 'Free the Penguins' demand. But her texts talk about Judgment Day, say everything has been arranged, and even mention an alarm. They are planning something, aren't they?"

Sarah turned to Sam. "Are they?"

Sam's lip quivered. She had tears in her eyes again. "I don't know," she said. "I don't! I like Frances a lot and believe in her cause – but this scares me."

"Me, too," said Travis.

"What do we do?" asked Sarah.

"What *can* we do?" Travis answered. "There's nothing here but talk. No one would listen to us. I say we go to the aquarium early and see if this is really the day they do the census."

"Maybe we can slip out right after breakfast," said Sarah. "We don't play until the afternoon."

"Okay. Just the three of us," said Travis. "If we see her and her group, and if we find out today's the day they do the census, we'd better tell someone."

"But tell them what?" said Sarah.

"Exactly," said Travis. "Which is why we'd better check things out before we make fools of ourselves. These texts are probably just gibberish."

"Or maybe not," said Sam. She started shaking again.

17

Immediately after breakfast, Travis, Sarah, and Sam slipped away. It wasn't difficult. Nish was telling a bunch of the other Owls that he and Data had a new invention: a hockey bag on wheels that you ran by remote control. Sarah didn't even waste time rolling her eyes as she hurried to the revolving doors on the side of the hotel closest to the New England Aquarium.

It was already 9:00 a.m., and the ticket line was lengthy. It was still the height of tourist season in Boston. A juggler was performing on the board-walk, surrounded by a large group of tourists who frequently applauded, but nowhere else could the three Owls see any sort of gathering.

They quickly rounded the back of the aquarium. Nothing there, either. Frances Assisi's text had said nothing about a specific place, just that they should meet at 9:00 a.m. sharp – that "arrangements" had been made.

They lined up for tickets. The line moved slowly, and Travis was glad of the distraction of the juggler. The juggler was extremely talented, but Travis could think of nothing but those cryptic messages received by Sam. What did they all mean? What was Judgment Day?

"We're next," Sarah said. She sounded out of breath, though for fifteen minutes they'd been almost standing still as the tourists – many of them in large groups – picked up their tickets.

"We're also late!" said Sam, who'd been growing ever more nervous.

"But for *what*?" Travis reminded them.

"Maybe nothing," said Sam. "I hope nothing."

So did Travis. From the moment he had met her, he hadn't liked this Frances woman. He didn't like the way she spoke to them, as if she was talking to people who weren't very bright and needed everything carefully explained. He didn't like the way she seemed to manipulate Sam, who had simply shown a love for the little penguins and now wouldn't eat meat of any sort and preached to the other Owls about animal cruelty. And he particularly didn't like the way Frances smiled with just her mouth while her eyes looked cold and cruel and calculating.

"Let's move it!" Sarah said, as she handed the tickets to her teammates. She turned and ran from the ticket booth to the aquarium's front doors, skirting ahead of a few slow-moving tour groups.

The three Owls were quickly inside.

It seemed a normal day at the aquarium in every way. The souvenir shop was already packed with people buying stuffed penguins and other mementos. There was a large crowd watching the feeding of the penguins, and one of the guides was giving a talk on the eating habits of the fascinating birds.

"The census would be done in the tank," Sarah said, tugging on Travis's sleeve. She moved quickly toward the ramps that took viewers on a circular path up and down the glass sides of the vast water tank.

Travis could see creatures swimming long before he got close. He saw a school of herring flash by like a thousand tiny mirrors in perfect time with each other. He could see other flashes of light as camera-carrying tourists chased after Myrtle the turtle, who passed window after window completely unaware of the gawking, excited tourists.

"We'll go to the top and then work our way back down," said Sarah. Travis and Sam nodded in agreement.

Half-running, dodging at times to get through the thick crowds, they were near the top of the gigantic tank when they rounded a corner and hit a wall of tourists listening intently to the New England Aquarium guide, Jocelyn, who had given the Owls their tour.

They had no choice but to stop. It would be too rude to push through. Sam bit her fingernails.

"So each year, we do a full count," Jocelyn was

saying. The guide had clearly been answering a question like the one Fahd had asked about the number of creatures in the tank.

"In fact," she continued. "This is day one of the annual census. Soon you will see divers entering the tank, and they will be conducting the count. It's very difficult work – can you imagine trying to count that school of herring accurately? – but it has to be done. They begin by category. Turtles are easy, and the divers get a totally accurate account of the larger fish, which they can tag. When it comes to the little guys, though, and the schools of fish, we do the count through photography and make certain calculations. We think we are pretty accurate."

"When do they start?" a young boy asked.

The guide turned to the window and looked down as well as she could through the curved glass into the lower depths of the tank.

"They've started," she said. "If you look down, you'll see quite a few divers are now in the tank."

The tourists pressed hard to the closest windows. The three Owls raced off to the side to find their own window.

Travis pressed so close to the glass his forehead left a mark.

"I see them!" said Sam.

"So do I!" said Sarah.

Travis watched, fascinated, as the divers, clad in wet suits and wearing fins and goggles and air tanks, slowly moved about the bottom of a reef-like structure that filled much of the tank, often picking up rocks in search of hidden creatures. They carried small counters, and a couple of the divers held what looked like computer tablets. Travis hoped they were waterproof.

The divers worked methodically, mostly staying at the bottom of the tank as they conducted their annual count.

But four divers were rising up from the bottom. Up and up they rose, carefully keeping it slow, their air bubbles racing ahead. Travis knew that ocean divers had to be careful not to come too quickly to the surface. Otherwise they could get the decompression sickness divers called the bends.

Travis watched them rise, the divers passing right by his window. He could see their equipment, including the gauges on their tanks that measured the amount of air time remaining.

Then he saw something that made his heart stop.

The diver passing closest by him, a woman, judging by the long hair flowing in the water, had her head turned slightly. She could not see him.

But for a brief moment, Travis could see her neck.

And there it was. The tattoo of a flying penguin.

18

The three Owls ran down the ramp as fast as they could. Several times they bumped into groups of tourists, some of whom yelled at them to slow down.

But Travis Lindsay couldn't slow down, any more than he could stop his heart pounding. He had an emergency message to deliver – just like Paul Revere!

They were almost at the bottom of the circular ramp when they saw a security guard. The man had seen them coming and was holding up his hand for them to halt.

But before he could say anything, the three young hockey players were sputtering and spewing out their story. None of which seemed to make the slightest sense to the guard.

"Hold on! Hold on!" he pleaded. "I can't make heads or tails of what you're saying. One at a time, please." He pointed at Travis. "You!"

Travis swallowed hard. He knew he'd have to be good. "We think there are people in your tank who shouldn't be there," he began.

The guard laughed. "You mean fish that shouldn't be there?"

"No, sir. We know one of the divers – and we don't think she should be there."

"Only authorized personnel are involved in any diving," the guard said. "So I doubt that very much."

Sam broke in. "She's Frances Assisi. The protester. The one behind the Free the Penguins movement."

This caught the guard's attention. He reached out and put a hand on Sam's shoulder. She was shaking, starting to cry again.

"You're certain of that?" he asked.

Sam nodded. "Yes. I know her very well. And she said she was planning something."

The guard took off his cap. He was sweating profusely under it, and his bald head shone in the lights of the aquarium. He seemed to be deciding what to do.

"Come with me," he said finally. "All three of you."

He turned and ordered the crowd behind them to make way for them to pass. Some of the people snickered to see the three youngsters being led away. They recognized them as the three who'd been running so recklessly down the ramp and were pleased the guard was doing the right thing by throwing the troublemakers out.

The guard was doing the right thing, sure enough – but it had nothing to do with giving the three Screech Owls the boot. He took them straight to the security office, where several guards were watching every area of the aquarium on video cameras, both inside and out.

The guard took them to a woman who appeared

to be the senior officer, and when Sam mentioned Frances Assisi's name, the woman's eyebrows jumped. They had her attention.

The senior officer turned to a bank of cameras focused on the tank itself. They could see sea creatures and divers moving about.

"Where?" she said to Travis. "Where in the tank did you see this?"

"Near the top," Travis said.

The senior officer nodded to another guard who had come over. "They go bottom to top for the census, don't they?"

"Yes, ma'am."

She turned to another guard operating the cameras. "Give us a view of the top of the tank, Peter."

Peter nodded. He pushed some buttons to control a camera positioned above the massive tank.

The four divers were working on something near the top of the reef-like structure. It did not look as if they were counting.

"Move in tight on this one," the senior officer said, tapping her finger on a figure with long hair flowing out of the hood of her wet suit.

The guard controlling the camera did so. The picture was a bit murky, but the Owls knew it was Frances.

"That her?" the senior officer asked.

All three Owls nodded at once.

The woman took one more look, straining to see what the divers were doing.

"Clear the building," she said.

The guard named Peter seemed unsure he'd heard correctly. "Ma'am?" he said.

"You heard me – clear the building. *Now!*"

19

Travis expected pandemonium, perhaps even people being trampled on the ramps. But there was nothing of the sort. A very calm announcement went out over the New England Aquarium's public-address system:

Security has detected a malfunction in the tank system. There is no need for panic, but all visitors must now clear the building temporarily. You will all be issued tickets for

readmission as you leave. Please exit the
building immediately in an orderly fashion.
We repeat: there is no need for concern.

The three Owls were also taken out, by the
security guard who had first stopped them. They
watched people leaving, lining up neatly outside
for their readmission tickets, and already Boston
police were on the boardwalk ensuring that the
crowds dispersed quickly and without incident.

Travis could tell from the passing voices that
there was indeed some concern – *"A leak?" "A break
in the glass?" "Something wrong in the water filtering
system?"* – but no one seemed to consider that this
was any sort of a Judgment Day.

The uniformed Boston police moved the
crowds back as a large armored bus rolled up and a
heavily armed police SWAT team poured out of it
and took up position around the outside of the
aquarium building. The security guard told the
Owls that SWAT stood for Special Weapons and
Tactics. This was the law enforcement unit that
handled only the most high-risk operations.

When the SWAT team was in place, a signal was given and they all entered the building at once, several of them going through the open side of the aquarium where the construction was taking place.

Sarah turned to the other two.

"*What if we're wrong?*" she asked, her face reddening.

Sam answered, "We're not."

20

"We have to go."

The security guard looked baffled. These three youngsters had caused one of Boston's top attractions to be evacuated and a SWAT team to storm the building. No one outside the New England Aquarium except them knew why, and now they had something *more important* to do?

"We have to," Sarah pleaded. "We play our final game of the tournament in an hour."

Quickly they explained to the guard, who had never even heard of the Paul Revere Peewee Invitational Hockey Tournament. He took down their details – their names, where they were staying, their home numbers – and raking a hand over his sweaty brow, he nodded that they were free to go.

They raced back to the hotel, arriving just as Mr. D was loading his portable skate-sharpening equipment onto the back of the old bus.

"*There* you are!" he shouted. "You three are running late! Grab your bags and get them down here. We leave in five."

The three Owls looked at each other. There was no time to tell anyone what had happened.

Besides, who would believe them anyway? And they didn't *really* know what had happened.

"Where the hell were you?" Nish said, as Travis sank into his stall in the dressing room at the TD Garden.

"We went to the aquarium again –"

"Bor-ing!" Nish said before Travis could continue.

Travis just smiled. He had no idea how to describe his morning, but *boring* was not one of the choices.

He put on his pads, right, left. All was quiet. He pulled his jersey over his head, kissed the Screech Owls crest from behind, and sagged in his stall. He was exhausted – and the final game still had to be played.

Travis could not recall a time when he'd been so out of it in a tournament. Was it just because it was summer? No – he'd been wrapped up in something else entirely. He had to get his focus back. *Had to*. He was captain, after all. He was Travis Lindsay, captain of the Screech Owls, and his teammates depended on him.

Their opponents in this final deciding match would be the Mini-Penguins. The Pittsburgh team, who'd been defeated by the Owls on Travis's goal and Nish's Hail Mary pass, had gone on to beat the Chicago Young Blackhawks 5–2, proving Muck's point that the Owls had found their game following that resounding opening loss to the Young Blackhawks.

Muck had little to say. His pregame talk set a new record for brevity.

"Have fun."

It was exactly the right thing for Muck to say. From Game 1, when the Owls had been humiliated, they had grown in confidence with every game, every shift. They were still far from mid-season form, but they were playing real hockey again, the game they loved so well.

And it *was* fun. It was fun when Travis pumped through that first corner on the fresh ice of the TD Garden. It was fun when he thought about being on the same ice that the Stanley Cup champions played on. It was fun when he hit the crossbar on his first warm-up shot. Fun when both Sarah and Sam slammed their sticks into his shin pads before the opening face-off. Fun when he and Nish did their ritual taps with Jenny, who'd be playing nets for the Owls. Fun when he came off from his first

shift and looked down the bench to see Nish lean-
ing over hard, his head buried between his knees.
Travis didn't need to see any more to know the
defenseman had his game face on.

The Mini-Penguins were going to be tough
again, perhaps even tougher than in the previous
match. The big center – the Lemieux-Crosby clone
– was in brilliant form, leading rush after rush up
the ice. Travis loved watching how effortlessly he
stickhandled, but he also knew it was his job to
ensure that the center's stickhandling didn't end up
with a puck in the net behind Jenny.

There was no score in the first period and,
amazingly, no score in the second. Muck always
argued that there could be nothing better than a
1–0 game in hockey, but Travis had never agreed
with that. Virtually every legendary game ever
played – the 1972 Summit Series, the 1987 Canada
Cup finals – had had the same score, 6–5, and he
figured any game with eleven goals had to be supe-
rior to a game with only one.

But this game was special.

The big center rushed often, but with Travis

staying back and Nish at the top of his game, they kept the big guy at bay, for the most part. And Sarah was on fire, skating as fast as or faster than any player on the ice.

The Owls were all playing their best. Fahd blocked shots. Simon Milliken put a beautiful check on the big Penguins' center. Jesse Highboy, never known for carrying the puck, rushed end to end and put a shot off the Penguins' goalpost. Jenny was superb in net, her glove hand lashing out like a cobra to bite off any shot that threatened to beat her.

Early in the third, the big center took a pass just over the red line and split Lars and Sam on defense. He came in hard on Jenny, dipped his shoulder to get her to make the first move, and then went backhand. But Jenny had refused to fall for the fake and was still standing there, the puck bouncing hard off her chest pad.

The puck bounced back, dropped, and skipped over Lars's stick and onto the stick of the Penguins' right winger, coming on fast in search of the rebound. He swung hard at the bouncing puck, coming in just under it, clipping it so it flew up, up, and over a helplessly falling Jenny.

The Mini-Penguins had the lead, 1–0.

Travis checked the clock. Twelve minutes left. The crowd, clearly many of them from Pittsburgh, were cheering hard for their heroes. Travis noticed a large number of waving American flags. No surprise. The Penguins were the American team, the Owls from Canada. And this was Boston, after all. Home of the Boston Tea Party, birthplace of the American Revolution. Patriotism here was huge.

"U.S.A.!" the crowd chanted.

"U.S.A.!"

"U.S.A.!"

Twelve minutes. Travis thought about it. More than enough time. But the clock seemed to be ticking faster and faster. Eleven. Ten. Less than ten minutes now . . .

Travis felt Muck's hand touch his shoulder and looked up. If Muck was anxious, he wasn't showing it. In fact, it struck Travis that Muck was loving this game, even if they were behind. And no doubt about it, it was a great game.

Travis leaped the boards as Derek came off. He checked the clock. Six minutes. Sarah had the puck in her own end and fed it off to Lars. Lars played a give-and-go with her, and Sarah broke over her own blue line, headed for center.

Dmitri was racing down the right side. Sarah put a perfect backhand pass off the boards and onto Dmitri's stick just before he crossed the Penguins' blue line.

Dmitri took the puck in and button-hooked it, pausing with it by the boards. As a defender came at him, he slipped the puck through the player's feet and Sarah caught it with her skates and kicked it up to her stick.

Travis knew his play. He rushed to the left of the net. If he crashed into the goalie, so be it – the important thing was to get to the net.

Sarah floated the pass to him. Travis hit it down out of the air and instantly cranked a hard shot – off the crossbar, over the glass, and into the crowd.

As they skated back to the bench, he slammed his stick down hard. Sarah cuffed the back of his legs with her stick.

"Nice try. Next time, we'll do it."

Travis nodded and sagged in his seat, gulping for breath. He checked the clock. Two minutes left.

Two minutes!

Muck signaled to Jenny that he wanted her high, out by the slot so she could get off fast if he called her.

Muck touched the back of Travis's neck. "Can you go again?"

Travis nodded, still gulping air.

The whistle blew, giving Travis a few more seconds of recovery time. Muck put out Nish and Lars together, the team's top defensemen, and then sent out Jesse, who'd been having another good game, and Andy, who could hold off the big center of the Penguins if needed.

Before the puck dropped, Nish glided along the boards by the Owls' bench.

He had something to whisper to Travis.

"Hail Mary!"

Travis nodded.

The Owls got the puck out and up over center, giving Muck the chance to wave Jenny to the bench and send Travis out as the extra attacker.

The crowd was bursting with excitement, every fan in the building rising to his or her feet.

The Mini-Penguins dumped the puck into the Owls' end, but not deep enough for an icing call.

Nish was first back, and he picked up the puck and stood with it behind the empty Owls' net. He looked calm as he surveyed the lie of the ice.

Travis knew what Nish was looking for. He spun hard and began skating down the left side, not even looking back to see what Nish would do next. He knew what Nish would do.

He was just about to reach the center ice line when he heard the crowd shout in surprise. He knew they were watching Nish's special play, the high Hail Mary pass that had worked so brilliantly before.

Travis listened for the puck to land beside him, knowing he was clear.

But there was no slap of the puck on the ice. *There was no puck!*

Instead, there was the sharp sizzle of other skates, and then the chop of skates skating away from him in the other direction.

He turned just in time to see the big center drop the puck down onto his own stick. He had intercepted Nish's Hail Mary!

Down the ice the big center flew, with Travis in pursuit. Only, Travis was now badly out of position. And Sarah, the only Owl fast enough to catch the center, was not on the ice to give chase.

It was all up to Lars and Nish. There was no goalie in the Owls' net, Jenny having been yanked so that Travis could go on.

Lars and Nish both fell in the hope of blocking the big center's shot, but the player held, danced the puck niftily between them, and very gently deposited the puck in the empty net.

Mini-Penguins 2, Owls 0.

The game was over, the championship lost.

21

In the dressing room, Travis was near tears. Had the big Mini-Penguin center not come over specially and tapped Travis on his pads, he might have openly wept. But he felt good about his game, and good about how far the Owls had come, for a team not used to summer hockey. You couldn't win every tournament.

Travis looked about. Sarah was staring at her skate laces. Sam was staring at the ceiling, seemingly in another world. Nish was bent over, gasping for air, his face hidden.

Muck was walking around the room, reaching down to touch each of the Owls on their shoulder. He didn't say a thing. He looked pleased rather than disappointed.

Mr. D came in, holding the door open behind him.

"Heck of a game, kids. Heck of a game. Travis, Sarah, Sam – you three get your stuff off and get outside. Someone wants to see you."

Travis looked at Sam, then at Sarah. They were suddenly back in the drama of the aquarium.

Travis fumbled with his skate laces, terrified that they had somehow messed up. Maybe he hadn't really seen the tattoo. Maybe it wasn't Frances. Maybe they had raised a false alarm.

"We owe you three, big time," the man was saying. He was the president of the New England Aquarium, but Travis wasn't even sure if he'd caught his name.

The man explained to them what had happened. Frances Assisi – real name Isobel Twining – and her group had somehow managed to infiltrate the diving crew that had been assigned to do the census. They had arranged for four identical diving outfits to be there for them when they got into the building and had somehow dressed without being noticed. The census takers thought they were staff divers; the staff divers thought they'd been brought in to help with the census.

The plan was alarmingly simple. And it might have been astonishingly successful, but for the three Owls.

Assisi and her three accomplices, the man explained, had been caught setting small boxes containing radio receivers at various levels in the tank. Once the receivers were in place, a radio signal from outside would set off a series of vibrations. If all the devices were completely in synch with each other, the vibrations would build until they shattered the glass windows.

The group had apparently tested their equipment at an isolated location and it had worked brilliantly, shattering glass thicker than that used in the aquarium. The radio signal was to be sent after the doors of the New England Aquarium had closed to the public. The plotters planned to call the aquarium security office five minutes before it happened, allowing time for workers still inside to clear the building of people.

"The idea was to 'flush' the aquarium creatures out into the harbor," the man told them. "When the glass shattered, it would send four stories of water — some two hundred thousand gallons — crashing down into the penguin display. Then that water, along with the tens of thousands of gallons of water in the penguin area, would burst through the opening in the wall at the construction site, sending the entire contents of the aquarium out into Boston Harbor."

"Free the penguins," Sam said under her breath. She sounded hurt. Hurt that she had ever been fooled into believing in whatever cause Frances thought they were fighting for.

Travis had a question. "Would all the creatures have escaped, then?"

The man shook his head. "Some would, of course, but most would have been killed by the collapsing tank. The entire penguin population would have been wiped out, for certain. They couldn't survive such a blow."

Travis nodded.

Free the penguins indeed.

22

The Screech Owls' bus rumbled back over the Thousand Islands Bridge, well on its way home to Tamarack. Travis hadn't slept yet on the long ride back, his mind churning again and again over the incredible events of their week in Boston.

He wasn't thinking much about the hockey tournament. He was thinking about how close Frances had come to destroying the New England Aquarium and killing all the innocent penguins she had wanted to "free." Perhaps the Owls had lost to the Mini-Penguins in the final, but the real penguins had won the game of their lives.

Travis and Sarah took great satisfaction from that, though Sam could not get it out of her head that she had fallen for Frances's fancy talk of freedom when the reality would have been destruction. They told Sam that she was really the hero of this story. It was only because she'd showed them those strange text messages – messages she was never meant to see – that the three had been able to disrupt the plan.

They had been interviewed by the police, but no newspaper or television reporters had learned of their involvement. The police had announced to the public that they had responded to warnings from "a source" and left it at that. The city had praised the police for their quick action and for ensuring that no one had been hurt, including the much-loved Myrtle the turtle, whose photo was on the front page of the *Boston Herald* Muck was reading on the way home.

The three Screech Owls were glad it had been kept quiet. Unlike Nish, they weren't interested in seeing their names in the papers unless it was about winning an Olympic medal someday — or the Stanley Cup.

Travis turned to look at his friend, who was sitting behind him, staring out the window, uncharacteristically quiet. What was Nish thinking? Muck had come by and told Nish to be ready to have a long talk with his mother when they got home. Mrs. Nishikawa was going to meet the bus. Nish was to tell her right away, Muck informed the troublesome young defenseman, that the postcard about quitting school was a bad joke and that Nish was looking forward more than ever to getting back to school in the fall.

Travis wondered how sincere Nish would be in saying that, but then he knew Nish could put on his choirboy face and look the picture of pure innocence. Nish would be at his acting best, he was sure.

As the bus rumbled on toward Nish's showdown with his mother, Travis finally started to doze off. A few minutes later, he was sound asleep.

"I have a new idea."

The quick breath tickling his ear woke Travis

up as much as the words. He sat up straight, blinking. Nish's face was right next to his ear.

"What's up?" Travis asked.

"Data 'n' me . . ."

"Data and I," Travis corrected.

"You're not involved. Data 'n' me have been thinking more about Ben Franklin's inventions. So many of them are completely obvious. He invented swim fins, did you know that? And the thing in your car that tells you how far you've gone . . ."

"They didn't have cars then," Travis protested sleepily.

"He had one on his carriage," Nish said dismissively, as if he couldn't believe Travis's lack of intelligence.

Nish continued. "He invented a new stove, new eyeglasses, an arm extension for reaching things . . . sensible stuff that people needed."

"You don't know the meaning of *sensible*."

Nish ignored him. "I've been thinking about something people really need but don't have."

"Which is?"

"Disposable underwear."

"What?"

"You guys are always complaining about my gauchies in the dressing room. My mom says she hates washing my underwear and is always on my case to change it every day – which is ridiculous."

"Not really."

"Well, my idea is simple, like Ben Franklin would do. You see a simple need, you find something sensible to fix it, and you're a genius."

"Disposable *underwear*?" Travis said.

"That's right – my latest invention. For hockey players like us."

Travis shook the rest of the sleep off. He needed to know if he was dreaming or if this conversation was actually taking place.

"You're too late," he said finally. "Somebody already came up with that."

"No way!"

"They're called diapers."

The last thing Travis heard before falling back to sleep was a persistent, hissing raspberry from the seat behind him.

**CHECK OUT THE OTHER BOOKS
IN THE SCREECH OWLS SERIES!**

THE MYSTERY OF THE RUSSIAN RANSOM

The Screech Owls have never had such a wonderful surprise. A famous Russian billionaire has offered to fly the whole team to his country, all expenses paid! The billionaire, a big supporter of Russian hockey, wants the Owls to visit his homeland so young hockey players can learn from the Screech Owls' style of play.

But before the team's first practice on the ice rinks of Ufa, Sarah is snatched off the snowy streets and taken captive. Her kidnappers say they want ten million rubles in exchange for her safe release. Yet why are they measuring and weighing and studying her like a laboratory rat? Will the billionaire pay the ransom, or will Travis and his friends decide to take matters into their own hands?

PANIC IN PITTSBURGH

Travis's memory must be playing tricks on him! Did he really hear that someone is going to steal the Stanley Cup?

The Owls have been invited to Pittsburgh to compete in the biggest hockey tournament ever to be played on outdoor ice. The open-air tournament is to be held in the massive Heinz Field arena, home of football's mighty Pittsburgh Steelers. But almost as soon as the tournament begins, Travis suffers a serious concussion, just like the injury that sidelined Penguins' superstar Sidney Crosby. Travis is confined to his hotel room so his injured brain can recover. His memory is patchy, and he's having some weird dreams. So when he stumbles upon an outrageous plot to steal hockey's most coveted trophy, he can't be sure if his mind is playing tricks or whether the danger is a terrible reality.

FACE-OFF
AT THE ALAMO

The Screech Owls are deep in the heart of Texas, in the southern city of San Antonio. The town is a surprising hotbed of American ice hockey, and the Owls are excited to come and play in the big San Antonio Peewee Invitational. Between games, they can explore the fascinating canals that twist and turn through the city's historic downtown.

The tournament has been set up to include guided tours of the Alamo, the world's most famous fort, where Davy Crockett fought and died. The championship-winning team will even get to spend a night in the historic fort.

The Screech Owls discover that the Alamo is America's greatest symbol of courage and freedom, and when Travis and his friends uncover a secret plot to destroy it, they must summon all the courage of the fort's original defenders.

THE NIGHT THEY
STOLE THE STANLEY CUP

Someone is out to steal the Stanley Cup – and only the
Screech Owls stand between the thieves and their prize!

Travis, Nish, and the rest of the Screech Owls have
come to Toronto for the biggest hockey tournament of
their lives – only to find themselves in the biggest *mess*
of their lives. First, Nish sprains his ankle falling down the
stairs at the CN Tower. Later, key members of the team get
caught shoplifting. And during a tour of the Hockey Hall
of Fame, Travis overhears two men plotting to snatch the
priceless Stanley Cup and hold it for ransom!

Can the Screech Owls do anything to save the most
revered trophy in the country? And can they rise to the
challenge on the ice and play their best hockey ever?

THE GHOST OF THE STANLEY CUP

The Screech Owls have come to Ottawa to play in the Little Stanley Cup Peewee Tournament. This relaxed summer event honors Lord Stanley himself – the man who donated the Stanley Cup to hockey – and gives young players a chance to see the wonders of Canada's capital city, travel into the wilds of Algonquin Park, and even go river rafting.

Their manager, Mr. Dillinger, is also taking them to visit some of the region's famous ghosts: the ghost of a dead prime minister, the ghost of a man hanged for murder, the ghost of the famous painter Tom Thomson. At first the Owls think this is Mr. Dillinger's best idea ever, until Travis and his friends begin to suspect that one of these ghosts could be real.

Who is this phantom? Why has he come to haunt the Screech Owls? And what is his connection to the mysterious young stranger who offers to coach the team?

SUDDEN DEATH IN NEW YORK CITY

Nish has done some crazy things – but nothing to match this! At midnight on New Year's Eve, he plans to "moon" the entire world.

The Screech Owls are in New York City for the Big Apple International Peewee Tournament. Not only will they play hockey in Madison Square Garden, home of the New York Rangers, but on New Year's Eve they'll be going to Times Square for the live broadcast of the countdown to midnight. It will be shown on a giant TV screen and beamed around the world by a satellite. Data and Fahd soon discover that, with just a laptop and video camera, they can interrupt the broadcast – and Nish will be able to pull off the most outrageous stunt ever.

Just hours before midnight, the Screech Owls learn that terrorists plan to disrupt the New Year's celebration. What will Nish do now? And what will happen at the biggest party in history?

PERIL AT THE WORLD'S BIGGEST HOCKEY TOURNAMENT

The Screech Owls have convinced their coach, Muck, to let them play in the Bell Capital Cup in Ottawa, even though it means spending New Year's away from their families. It's a chance to skate on the same ice rink where Wayne Gretzky played his last game in Canada, and where NHLers like Daniel Alfredsson, Sidney Crosby, and Mario Lemieux have played.

During the tournament, political leaders from around the world are meeting in Ottawa. To pay tribute to the young hockey players, the prime minister has invited the leaders to watch the final game on New Year's Day. The Owls can barely contain their excitement!

Meanwhile, as Nish is nursing an injured knee off-ice, he may have finally found a way to get into the *Guinness World Records*. But what no one knows is that a diabolical terrorist also has plans to make it a memorable – and deadly – game.

ROY MacGREGOR was named a media inductee to the Hockey Hall of Fame in 2012, when he was given the Elmer Ferguson Memorial Award for excellence in hockey journalism. He has been involved in hockey all his life, from playing all-star hockey in Huntsville, Ontario, against the likes of Bobby Orr from nearby Parry Sound, to coaching, and he is still playing old-timers hockey in Ottawa, where he lives with his wife, Ellen. They have four grown children. He was inspired to write *The Highest Number in the World*, illustrated by Geneviève Després, when his now grown-up daughter started playing hockey as a young girl. Roy is also the author of several classics in hockey literature. *The Home Team: Fathers, Sons and Hockey* was shortlisted for the Governor General's Award for Literature. *Home Game: Hockey and Life in Canada* (written with Ken Dryden) was a bestseller, as were *Road Games: A Year in the Life of the NHL*, *The Seven A.M. Practice*, and his latest, *Wayne Gretzky's Ghost: And Other Tales from a Lifetime in Hockey*. He wrote *Mystery at Lake Placid*, the first book in the bestselling, internationally successful Screech Owls series in 1995. In 2005, Roy was named an Officer of the Order of Canada.